The Secret Life of Lincoln Jones

Also by Wendelin Van Draanen

How I Survived Being a Girl
Flipped
Swear to Howdy
Runaway
Confessions of a Serial Kisser
The Running Dream

The Sammy Keyes Mysteries

Sammy Keyes and the Hotel Thief
Sammy Keyes and the Skeleton Man
Sammy Keyes and the Sisters of Mercy
Sammy Keyes and the Runaway Elf
Sammy Keyes and the Curse of Moustache Mary
Sammy Keyes and the Hollywood Mummy
Sammy Keyes and the Search for Snake Eyes
Sammy Keyes and the Art of Deception
Sammy Keyes and the Psycho Kitty Queen
Sammy Keyes and the Dead Giveaway
Sammy Keyes and the Wild Things
Sammy Keyes and the Cold Hard Cash
Sammy Keyes and the Wedding Crasher
Sammy Keyes and the Night of Skulls
Sammy Keyes and the Power of Justice Jack
Sammy Keyes and the Showdown in Sin City
Sammy Keyes and the Killer Cruise
Sammy Keyes and the Kiss Goodbye

SECRET *the* LIFE of LINCOLN JONES

Wendelin Van Draanen

Alfred A. Knopf
New York

THIS IS A BORZOI BOOK PUBLISHED BY ALFRED A. KNOPF

Knopf, Borzoi Books, and the colophon are registered trademarks of Penguin Random House LLC.

Visit us on the Web! randomhousekids.com

Educators and librarians, for a variety of teaching tools, visit us at RHTeachersLibrarians.com

Library of Congress Cataloging-in-Publication Data is available upon request.
ISBN 978-1-101-94040-2 (trade) — ISBN 978-1-101-94041-9 (lib.bdg.) —
ISBN 978-1-101-94042-6 (ebook)

The text of this book is set in 12.5-point Chaparral Pro.

Printed in the United States of America
October 2016
10 9 8 7 6 5 4 3 2 1

First Edition

For the angels

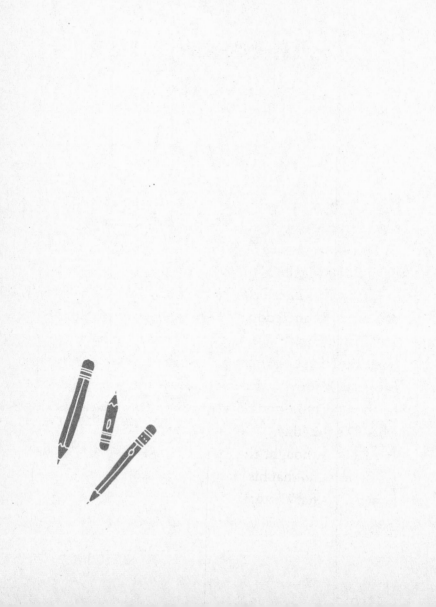

1

An Unexpected Blow

Ruby Hobbs came out of her room, dancing and singing, buck naked, again. *"All I want is a room somewhere, far away from the cold night air,"* she warbled, her old body jigglin' and wigglin'.

Ruby being naked may sound funny, but it's a sight so disturbing even Teddy C can't take it, and that's saying something. Teddy C ogles all the oldies. Fat ones, bony ones, doesn't seem to matter to him. He's ninety, but his eye is always roving. He does the whistle, too. Or at least he tries. It's more air than sound, but there's no mistaking what he's thinking.

At first I thought the whistle was a joke, but Ma says it's for real and that his old-guy eyes see what they used to know, not what's actually there.

Except, I guess, in the case of Ruby Hobbs. "Somebody help!" Teddy C called, like he was being robbed. "She's at it again!"

"Now, now, dear," Gloria said, snatching a sheet from one of the monster-eye dryers and rushing over to wrap Ruby in it. "You can't dance at the ball without a gown on. What would the governor think?"

Gloria sure does have a way with the oldies. Maybe it's how she can jump inside whatever fantasy or memory they're in the middle of. Or maybe it's the fake flower she wears in her hair. It's the exact same one every day, but every day it seems brand-new to the folks living at Brookside. "Oh, what a beautiful bloom!" someone'll say, like it's the first time they've seen it. "As pretty as you," Gloria'll reply, which makes them blush. Like it's the first time they've been paid the compliment.

It could also be the way Gloria's voice always seems to calm things down. Her *now, now*s and *there, there*s work like she's castin' a spell.

Whatever it is about Gloria, her magic doesn't only work on the oldies. It works on me, too. Ma tells me, "Focus," but all I can think about is how dumb it is that I have to spend my afterschools here, in an old-folks' home.

Gloria, though, will give me a little smile and whisper, "Now, now, Lincoln. Remember, the more schoolwork you get done here, the less you'll have to do when you get home," and just like that, I buckle down.

But back to Ruby.

I'd been coming to Brookside every school day since September, and even though we were in the middle of November, it was still a surprise to see Ruby bust out her dance moves. Aside from her being naked, which I guess anyone can figure out how to get, the big shock is always seeing her *move.*

Normally she shuffles. *Shuff, shuff, shuff,* her slippers go. *Shuff, shuff, shuff,* slow and tired. All the oldies shuffle. Usually with walkers, or while hanging on the arm of one of the nurses. Or, I guess, "caregivers." The word seems so stiff, but Ma says I need to use it, seeing how caregivers are not actually nurses. At Brookside, nurses are the ones in white shirts, and caregivers are the ones in purple shirts. Nurses do the pills and the blood pressure and call the ambulance. Caregivers do the meals and the clothes and all the nasties. Like mopping up accidents. And changing diapers. And dressing corpses.

But back to shufflin'.

It's what all the oldies do. Going to the Clubhouse at mealtimes, to the Activities Room for entertainment hour, to the patio for a little afternoon sun . . . they shuffle and they look straight down at the floor. It's easy to get lulled into how *slow* everything goes. Which is why Ruby coming out of her room naked with her arms out and twirling is always such a shock.

This time, though, it was different.

This time, the flower and the sunny sounds from Gloria didn't help. Ruby cried when Gloria wrapped her up, and she whimpered, "Let me dance. Please. Let me dance."

This time, seeing Ruby Hobbs was more than just surprising or disturbing or funny. It was sad. And sad on top of everything else that had happened was an unexpected blow. One that knocked the wind right out of me.

2

Spinnin' Lies into Truth

The trouble at my new school began the very first day, during the very first recess. It's bad enough starting a new school when everybody else acts like they've known each other since diapers. And it's bad enough when your new teacher makes everyone read a passage aloud from a story and then fusses over your "darling Southern accent." Ms. Miller thought she was payin' me a compliment, but no boy, sixth-grade or otherwise, wants to be put in the same sentence as "darling."

But worse is recess, when you've got nowhere to go. It's time-tickin' torture. Ms. Miller had instructed us to "stay within the confines of the blacktop area for today." I had no interest in making a further fool of myself by handling a ball, so I went to go sit in the shade of a tree off the edge of the blacktop. And I was just fixin' to sit down when I noticed a stream of miniature black ants windin' around the tree's trunk. I stayed standing, studying them. They were nothing like the ants back home—those ants could haul a house away. These were small as fleas, scurryin' up and down in a thin, winding line.

"Hey!" a kid on the playground called. "We use bathrooms in these here parts!"

The voice seemed off in the distance, barely reaching my mind 'cause I was concentrating on ants.

"Hey!" he called again. "Quit whizzin' on the tree!"

What he was sayin'—and that his fake Southern accent was aimed right at me—hit like a bolt of lightning. I whipped around quick. I didn't know him, but he was standin' near the edge of the playground with a boy I recognized from my class.

"I was just lookin' at ants!" I hollered, but it was too late. They ran off, hee-hawin' like donkeys.

Back in class, Hee-Haw #2 spread it around to the guys on his side of the room. I could see them grinnin' and whisperin', spinnin' lies into truth. It was the first day of school and already the beginning, middle, and end of any hope I had for making new friends.

After that I took to hiding out. It was a whole lot safer than opening myself up to the hazards of a new school full of old friends. If they could make such a fuss over me watching ants, I didn't want to find out what they'd do if they knew where I went after school.

3

The Fling Zone

It didn't take long to settle into the new routine. I ride the school bus to Thornhill School in the mornings and the city bus home from Brookside after Ma's shift is done at night. To get from school to Brookside, I walk. It's only about twelve blocks, but it's a long twelve blocks when you're tired from school and luggin' a backpack and you're on your way to a home for oldies. It's not exactly a destination to look forward to when you're eleven.

Or even when you're ninety, now that I think about it.

If I dawdle, I hear about it from Ma. "What took you?" she whispers, giving a worried look at the wall clock. "You're not getting mixed up in anything, are you?"

"Ma-ah," I groan, 'cause I've *never* been mixed up in anything. Her asking me that came on after we moved. Maybe 'cause we're living in a "rough zone," as she calls it, but our apartment is a long ways from the route I walk from school to Brookside, so her frettin' like she does makes no sense to me.

Finally, she'll see that I'm just tired and hungry and say, "Let's get you a snack."

Snacks at Brookside are okay. Not great, but okay. They're for old folks, so they're low in fat and sugar and salt, which adds up to them being low in flavor, too. They're still better than the snacks marked *D*, which are for the diabetics and made with fake sugar, since real sugar could send them into a diabetic coma.

But the snacks are free and the juice is usually cold, which is mostly what matters. And after I'm parked at my regular table with my snack, Ma can quit worrying about me and what I might have been doing on the walk over and get back to work.

I don't tell her this, but it's not the walk she should be worrying about.

It's the bus.

I don't mean the city bus, either. She's with me on that one, so she knows what I see there. She always has advice for me when we're on it, too. "Don't stare, Lincoln," she'll whisper. "He's drunk."

Like I haven't seen drunk enough to recognize it? Like I haven't figured out it's the whole reason she dragged me halfway across the country? I know drunk, and I can usually ditch drunks. Ma . . . well, that's a different story.

But back to the bus.

On the city bus, we're allowed to sit anywhere. We can move away from trouble if it starts up, and that makes the city bus a safe zone compared to the school bus.

The rule on the school bus is little kids up front, big kids in back. And the first couple of weeks I followed that rule because it made sense to me.

Besides, what sixth grader wants to sit with first graders?

Before we moved, I used to walk to school, so I never knew how rough the back of a school bus can get. Ma doesn't want me watching R movies or playing violent video games, but the back of a school bus is as bad as both.

Usually when there's trouble brewin', I find a way to sidestep it. I hush up, duck out, and live to see another day. So that's what I tried to do on the school bus. I started bending the seating rule a little, not going all the way back when we piled on. I'm not exactly big for eleven, and I'm new, so the younger kids didn't really know any different, and they didn't seem to mind.

But the kids at the back of the bus sure did.

"Dude, ain't you in Miller's class? Why you sitting way up there?"

"Yeah, whatsa matter? You got a problem with us?" It was Hee-Haw #1. The one who wasn't in my class.

I waved at them like, no hard feelings, but I guess there were hard feelings anyway, 'cause as the bus roared along, the teasing started. First they picked on my "drawl" and how I was "a Southern boy." Then the names began flyin'. Hee-Haw #1 started off callin' me the Wiz, but one of his herd thought that was a cool name—like I was smarter'n them, or a wizard. So he moved on pretty quick from that to messin' with my name, calling me the Missing Link and the Weak Link and then just Link for short.

I knew they were trying to make me *say* something so they could make fun of the way I'd said it, but what it did instead was make me face forward and keep my mouth shut tight. But over time the names went from mean to meaner, 'til they were so bad I'd've been whupped to Sunday if I'd said them at home.

When they ran out of new names, they added shoving.

And when they got bored of the shoving, they added spitting.

By October they were up to spoon flinging. I got hit with grape bombs and tuna fish and Jell-O and whatever part of some other kid's lunch they didn't mind wasting. They were sly about it, so the bus driver never saw them, and everyone else was too afraid to do anything. Instead of trying to get rid of the flingers, the little kids tried to get rid of me. "You can't sit here," they told me, and who could blame them? I was the target, but with spoon flingin' there's lots of hits outside the bull's-eye.

I didn't know what to do about it. It's not like I could tattle. I knew where that'd get me. And it's not like I could change my mind and start sitting further back. Either way, I'd get murdered.

So I was stuck.

Stuck in the fling zone, with tuna in my hair.

4

The Great Escape

Maybe I was willin' to put up with tuna and Jell-O flying at me 'cause they were nothing compared to what I'd been hit with before the move. For Ma it was even worse.

Then on New Year's Eve almost a year ago, Ma made a resolution: we were moving.

Escaping Cliff.

Starting over.

She whispered it to me with a bloody lip and a puffy eye while I was in my hiding place, under my bed.

Ma's escape plan included stashing away cash, which meant meager eats and no extras for a good six months. It also included two small duffels and two one-ways on the Greyhound bus.

The night of the great escape I didn't sleep a wink. I had my duffel packed light, like Ma had told me—spare clothes, travelin' food, and a toothbrush, plus the only things I couldn't stand leaving behind: my secret notebooks.

When it was finally time, we walked the three miles to the station like our unders were on fire. In some ways they were, 'cause it was late July and swelterin', even at five in the morning.

Ma kept looking over her shoulder, but we made it to the station without being stopped. The only worry I had was the worry I caught from Ma, who was oozing with it. The way I saw it, Cliff was on whiskey time. He wouldn't be up 'til noon.

I'll never forget Ma's face, reflectin' in the bus window as we pulled out of the station. She didn't know I could see or she'd have hid it better, but she was one scared rabbit. "Oh, Lord," she whispered, clutchin' her bag tight. "Lord, oh, *Lord*."

She may have been scared out of her mind, but I was glad to get gone. After Cliff moved in with us, our life turned into a bad movie that got played over and over, with the fight scenes getting longer and louder.

Cliff wasn't just mean to Ma. After I called him out on a couple of lies, he took to hating me. The older I got, the meaner he got, so leaving didn't scare me near as much as staying did.

Plus, I was looking forward to meeting my aunt Ellie and my cousin Cheyenne. I figured they had to be nice, seeing how they were letting us stay with them until Ma could find a job and a place of our own.

But then we arrived.

It probably doesn't matter how nice a person is—when the apartment's small, two more bodies get in the way quick. And Aunt Ellie pushed Ma's buttons in a big way. Ma tried to explain it to me one night, keepin' her voice hushed as we camped out in the front room. "It's like we're kids again, with her bossing and criticizing and making me feel worthless!"

"Better'n gettin' beat up," I whispered back.

She muttered something but wouldn't repeat it, and it took me 'til after she was sleeping to figure out that she'd said, "Just a different kind of beat up, is all."

So Ma had problems with her sister, and it didn't take but a day or two for me to start having them with Cheyenne. She was in high school, so she got over the excitement of meeting her long-lost cousin before I was done stepping through the door. And the bathroom was definitely *hers*. Plus, she wore morning on her sleeve like a gaping wound. I swear that girl could not smile before two p.m., and by then I was too worn out from watching my step to be any kind of friendly.

"We have *got* to get out of here," Ma said after a few weeks, and I guess Aunt Ellie and Cheyenne agreed, because the instant Ma landed the job at Brookside, Aunt Ellie offered to loan her the money we needed to rent a place of our own.

The apartment we moved to is above a corner market, and it's small.

Smaller'n small.

To get to it is strange, too. First you go through a metal gate, then you go down a kind of alleyway to some metal stairs that go up to an outside hallway. Our apartment is marked *A*, and there's another door further down marked with a dangling *B*.

Our place has one bedroom and one bathroom with a toilet, a sink, and a small metal-basin shower with a wrap-around curtain. There's one plug-in burner on top of the half-sized fridge near the kitchen sink, and a two-person table off to the side of the front room, where my mattress is parked in a corner. Ma gets the bedroom, which isn't much bigger than a closet, and the only heat is from the plug-in burner.

We gave the place a Pine-Sol bath when we moved in, and when we were sitting down to jelly sandwiches that first night, Ma apologized and said, "I know it's not much, but we'll fix it up."

"I like it fine," I told her, which was the truth. I had my little corner, and we were inside our own walls. Nobody was going to be bargin' in angry or drunk or even just annoyed.

I knew it was a dump. I knew I could have hated it. But the weird thing is, even from that first night, it felt like home.

5

Kandi Kain

When Ms. Miller called Kandi Kain's name the first day of class, I thought for sure it was a joke. Maybe some kind of play on her real name that had caught on. But I learned later that Kandi Kain carries around a copy of her birth certificate just so she can set the record straight for any nonbelievers.

When I saw the certificate, all worn out from being flashed around since probably kindergarten, I became a different kind of nonbeliever.

What sort of mama gives her girl a name like that?

"My mother said it makes me unforgettable," Kandi said, the words flowin' out like warm maple syrup. "And it was better than naming me Nova, right? Or Hurra."

"Hurra's not a name," I said.

She hoisted an eyebrow at me. "And Link is?"

I frowned. "It's Lincoln," I told her, and it came out kinda proud-sounding.

Like the way Ma always says it.

Kandi was not impressed. Or convinced. "So you say," she oozed. Then she gave me a scary-sweet smile. "Can you prove it?"

"Prove what?"

"That your name's Lincoln. How do we know you're not just making that up?"

"Why would I go makin' up a name?"

"You thought I did, didn't you?"

"But your name is Kandi Kain!"

"And yours is Lincoln Jones." She gave me a cool look. "The more I think about it, the more I think you made it up. No mother names her child Lincoln. Besides, it doesn't fit with Jones." She turned her nose up a little. "Jones is ordinary. Lincoln is pretentious."

I didn't know what *pretentious* meant, but I sure didn't like the way it sounded. Like I was pretendin' to be something I wasn't. And her nose bein' up like it was didn't help, either. So I let her have it. "Ma says my names balance each other. And that Lincoln is an honorable name. One I should be proud of."

"Hmm," she said, considering me. "I guess that's true."

Darn straight! I thought, and for a second I felt good.

But then she went and said, "But 'Ma'? You really call your mom that? Where *are* you from, anyway?"

Ma always tells me that the best way to get rid of a pest is to ignore it. "If you swat at the bee, Lincoln, it'll surely sting you." And having been stung by a bee a time or two, I know she's right. But sittin' around waiting for the thing to fly off on its own is terrifying. There it is, walking on you, all fuzzy and twitchin', with its stinger fixin' to fire, while you sit holding your breath, sweating bullets.

Still, any time I've managed to not swat, I haven't been stung. I remind myself of that fact when tuna's flingin' at me on the bus. I don't swat at the pests on the bus, and I don't swat at them in the classroom.

It's hard, but that's what I do.

Now, Kandi Kain may not fling tuna, but she's still dangerous 'cause she's got that queen bee thing going on. She likes swarms of kids around her. Boys *and* girls. She holds the four-square balls hostage at recess, then directs kids around, and for some reason they do what she says. She's pretty, sure, but that's no reason for folks to act like drones.

So I kept my distance and did my own thing, but every time she'd look at me, there'd be a frown bendin' down her face. Then, one day in early October, she marched right up to me and said, "What's with you and that notebook? You writing the Declaration of Independence, or what?"

Her hands were on her hips, showin' off fingers that were painted like candy corn—yellow at the base, orange in the middle, and white at the tip. I could tell her joke about the Declaration of Independence had been brewing in her brain for some time. I could tell she thought it was smart and clever, too. Like sportin' candy-painted nails when your name is Kandi.

Too bad for her, I just thought it was dumb. "Abraham Lincoln had nothing to do with the Declaration of Independence," I told her. "He came almost a hundred years later."

That hushed her up for one whole blink of the eye.

"So what are you writing, then?"

I'd already closed the notebook when I'd seen her coming over.

I'm not stupid.

"Nothing," I told her, 'cause that's what I tell everybody when they ask. It's not rude. It's universal for *none of your business.*

But I guess when the universe revolves around you, things work a different way. "Of course you're writing something," she said. "Don't need to get all huffy about it."

"I wasn't gettin' huffy!" I said, and it came out so huffy my cheeks started to burn.

She gave me one of those scary-sweet smiles, then twitched up an eyebrow and said, "So you drawing pictures of me, or what?"

"No!" I cried, and slapped open my notebook. "It's just stories, see?"

She nosed right in, and her eyes seemed to be gulping up the words. "Annie?" she asked, pointing a candy-corn nail at the name. "Are you writing about Annie Totes?"

I gave her a blank look. Who was Annie Totes?

"In our class?" she asked.

I felt like a double fool. "No!" I slapped the notebook closed again. "It's nobody." And then, 'cause I could tell she didn't believe me, I let on a little. "The Annie in my story's a character, all right? She's an old lady."

"Like somebody's grandmother?"

"Yeah, like that," I said, even though it wasn't like that at all.

"So what's she doing?"

I stared at her a second, and for that second it felt like she wasn't just being nosy. It felt like she really wanted to know. And in that second, I was dying to tell her all about Annie and the hero of the story, Lamar, and his pet wolf, Howler, and how Annie was being haunted by chain-rattlin' ghosts.

And then that second passed and I came to my senses.

"Nothin'," I said, and put the notebook away.

6

Classmates

Not knowing who Annie Totes was was part of a problem I didn't know I had until it was too embarrassing to fix. I'd been so busy puttin' my head down and avoidin' folks that I hadn't bothered learning the names of the kids in my class. That's okay the first day or first week or even the first couple of weeks of school, but a month in, it was all-at-once embarrassing.

As in when Ms. Miller asked me to hand back papers and I couldn't. And when I slipped up on the Annie Totes question.

It's not like I knew *nobody*. There was Kandi, of course, and I'd figured out the Hee-Haws. The one in my class was named Hank, and the one who was on the bus and in the other sixth-grade class was named Ryan. Hank didn't mess with me in class and he didn't ride my bus, but when he got with Ryan at recess, it was like flippin' a switch.

I also knew Benny Tazmin. He's no bigger'n me, but he fills the room with his jokes and snickers. Remembering his name came easy 'cause Ms. Miller's on him a lot for "disruptive behavior," and the boys around him egg him on, cheering, "Ben-ny, Ben-ny!" or they tattle on him, saying, "It was Taz!"

Besides Kandi and Benny and Hank, I also knew the two girls who were always trailing after Kandi. The reason I knew their names was because Kandi acts like she's supervising them and does it using both their names like a parent: "Lexi Simmons, where have you been?" "Macy Mills, are you coming or not?" The three of them seem to be in some sort of fashion club that moves from stripes to polka dots to solids and back, and involves socks with animal designs. One of them's always messin' up in the eyes of the others, though, and half the time it seems they don't even like each other. Maybe they do and have a funny way of showin' it. Maybe they should stick to simpler socks.

And then there were my tablemates, Colby, Rayne, and Wynne. All girls. Colby's bossy, with a nose that's usually tipped up and twitchin' like she's trackin' someone's scent. Rayne's shy, with a lion's mane of dark hair, and Wynne wears wire-rimmed glasses and whispers everything, always.

So out of the twenty-eight kids in class, I knew nine.

And that included me.

That afternoon, though, it bumped up to ten when Kandi caught my eye and did a big point-point with a candy-corn finger at a girl across the classroom. She shielded her pointing hand with her other hand but didn't come anywhere near covering what she was doing. And then she mouthed a big, exaggerated "ANNIE TOTES!" that anyone could see.

I covered my face and slumped in my chair.

Kandi Kain is the worst.

7

Followed

What I thought about Kandi was proven true on my walk to Brookside that same afternoon. "Where *are* you going?" a voice right behind me said.

It made me jump, and when I whipped around, sure enough, I was face to face with Kandi.

"You take the twenty-seven bus *to* school," she panted. "But you walk this way after. And you keep on walking forever! Where are you going?"

I didn't notice I was being followed 'cause sometimes when I get to thinking about my stories, everything else sort of blanks out. In this case I was in the middle of a big fight scene in my head where Lamar and Howler corner the guy who's been faking the chain-rattlin'-ghost stuff. His name's Mr. Butte and he's meaner'n skunk spray. And now that he's trapped in the corner of a basement, he's desperate.

I like playing out scenes in my head before I write them. I'll do the same scene over and over on my way to Brookside, fine-tuning it 'til I'm itching to put it on paper. My favorite is when I get to a scene near the end of a story where the villain is trapped in a basement, or pinned in an alleyway, or tossed headfirst inside a jail cell. I live for the clank of a jail cell. Doesn't matter if the story is turning out good or bad, I finish just so I can hear the jail cell slammin' shut.

Ma doesn't get why I'm always scribblin' in a notebook. "It's not a journal?" she asked after I'd filled up the first one and was starting on a second.

"No, ma'am," I told her. "It's stories."

"Like . . . made-up stories?"

"Yes, ma'am."

She studied me for a bit. "So it's not private, then? I can read it?"

But I didn't let her. I worried that she'd say how wonderful they were because she's my ma, or that I'd be able to tell from her face they weren't any good. Either way, I didn't want her to see. I didn't want *anyone* to see.

But back to Kandi sneaking up on me.

I didn't notice it 'cause I was a long ways from school and my mind was with Lamar and Howler, down in a dark, eerie basement cornering evil Mr. Butte. That, and I don't happen to have eyes in the back of my head.

I was mad at Kandi for spooking me, and even madder

at *me* for getting spooked. And on top of getting mad and madder, I got an instant case of the worries. We were half a block from Brookside, and I sure couldn't have Kandi knowing I spent my afters at an old-folks' home!

I stopped walking. "Why you followin' me?"

"Where are you going?" she asked, like her questions mattered way more than mine. "There's nothing back this way!"

My mind was scrambling. "Well, there must be, or I wouldn't be headed this way, right?"

"So where, then?"

I was stuck. And I was mad. And my mouth kept right on being stupid. "To the intersection of Nowhere and None of Your Business," I said. "And how do you know I take the twenty-seven?"

She looked down. "Hilly's on the twenty-seven. She says Troy's pretty mean to you."

I knew which one Troy was, but Hilly? I gave Kandi a good, hard squint. "Who?"

"Hillary Howard? She's in Mr. Ulman's sixth with Troy. Short brown hair. Bracelets?"

I rolled my eyes. "Oh, her." Then I gave another good, hard squint. "Why's she sit with him if she thinks he's mean?"

Kandi looked away. "Being a girl is . . . complicated."

Like that was any kind of answer?

Then real quick she switched subjects. "But the twenty-seven picks up on the west side, and you're going due east."

"Am I?" I said, 'cause I had no idea what direction I was

headed, and hearing "due east" come out of someone with such long, shiny hair and fingernails painted like candy corn just seemed . . . strange.

"Sun's over there," she said, pointing behind us, then nodded in the direction I was headed. "So that's east."

"Well, doesn't matter which direction I'm goin'," I said. "You've got no business following me."

"Look," she said, "I've got to get home. I just wanted to make sure you're okay."

I stared at her, thinkin' that if lies were flames, she'd be one towerin' inferno.

My dark look didn't seem to affect her, though. She danced off with a little wave and called, "Tell Annie and Howler I say hi!"

"Howler's a *wolf*," I yelled after her.

"I know that!" she called back.

Which left me kinda dumbstruck.

How could she have picked that up from one little look at the page?

It didn't help my case of the worries, that's for sure. I headed on toward Brookside, wonderin' if she could read *me* just as easy.

8

The Crazies

Going inside Brookside is like pushing through a secret revolving door. On one side there's daylight and trees and cars and *movement*.

On the other there's Death.

They try to cover that up with soft music playing and a big lobby that looks like it's straight out of a magazine. I never sit there myself, and nobody else seems to use it, either. It's like a big, fancy family room missin' its family, and if you hold still in it for even just a minute, you can feel Death lurking nearby.

Even so, I was glad to step inside. Kandi might have been long gone, but her following me still had me jittery.

"Good afternoon, Lincoln! Isn't it a lovely day?" the receptionist said, shooing Death away. She's told me lots of times to call her Geri, but I was still having trouble doing that.

"Yes, ma'am. It sure is," I said as I went up to her desk.

She smiled as I signed in. "You have got to be the politest boy I've ever met."

"Ma'am?"

She stood. "We're not used to being *ma'am*'d around here, but I must say, I do enjoy it." Her heels clicked on the tile floor as she led the way across the lobby to the East Wing, which is the side where Ma works. She raised an eyebrow in my direction. "My grandson calls me dude."

Being reminded that I talk different from other folks around here had me feelin' all self-conscious. Ma says I just need to start putting the *g*'s on my words—something she's been working hard at since her sister told her, "You sound like a hick," when we were staying with her and Cheyenne. Ma fumed about it for days, but now she's correctin' *my* speech. At supper the other day she even told me that sayin' "ma'am" was "regional" and that I should maybe go easy on it. I dropped my fork. After years of drillin' it into my head, she wants me to go easy on it?

But back to being walked across the lobby.

Anyone can come into the lobby. But if you want to get to the rooms where the oldies roam, you have to sign in and someone has to let you in.

Someone also has to let you out.

Mounted on both sides of every main doorway is an entry keypad, and the folks who work at Brookside are sly about shielding the pad with one hand as they type in the secret code with the other. They're chatty while they do it, so it feels like they're playing a shell game—sly shuffling moves mixed with small talk to trick you into forgetting what's where.

I usually look away from the keypad because I know it's the polite thing to do, and I always go along with the small talk, but I never forget that once you've been shuffled in, you can't come out without the secret code.

Even Ma won't tell me the combination. "I'm not about to jeopardize my job," she said when I asked. "And you're never there without me, so you have nothing to worry about."

It still made me feel trapped. So I asked, "What if there's a fire and everyone but me's in Activities?"

"Hush, Lincoln."

"But what if—"

"Lincoln, I'm not telling you!"

So one time while Geri was letting me in, I did the sly-eye and got the combination myself. I've felt safer ever since.

But back to Geri walking me across the lobby.

She was thumbing in the code, talking about the weather, when an oldie's face popped up in the East Wing's door window.

"Oh, dear," Geri said, because it was Suzie York, looking

like a pitiful dog begging to get out. "We'd better go through Activities."

I used to think you could talk your way past Suzie York, but it's tough 'cause she's stuck in an endless loop of finding a way out. So when Geri did a U-turn back across the lobby, I was all for it, even though it was the long way around.

Activities is a really big room between the East and West Wings. Everything from exercise classes to movies to crafts happens in Activities. You can get to it from the lobby, the courtyard, or either of the wings, but from any direction you need the secret code to get inside.

So Geri keyed us in and detoured me through Activities, past the tables and chairs, which were all shoved to one side so a man with a big roll-around bucket could mop the floor. "Enjoy your afternoon," she told me as she let me into the East Wing through a side door.

"Yes, ma'am," I said, then went down a corridor, past a side hallway with a fake street sign saying DOVE LANE, and to the Clubhouse, which is what they call the big room where the East Wing oldies eat or hang out when they're not sleeping.

It's also the place I spend my afters.

Before I could make it to my usual table, though, Suzie York cornered me with sad puppy-dog eyes and said, "Where'd you come from? How'd you get in? Can you get me out?"

"Sorry, Mrs. York," I told her. "Only your family can get you out."

She gave me a puzzled look. "How do you know my name?"

"Oh, we've met before."

She glossed right over that and got back to what she really wanted to know. "Where'd you come in?"

"Down the hall," I said, keepin' it vague.

"Which hall? Where? Does it lead outside?"

Just then another lady, Debbie Rucker, shouted, "What is your name?" from across the room.

I knew she was talking to me.

She does the same thing every single solid day.

"Don't yell!" Suzie yelled, which only made Debbie yell it louder. "What is your name?!"

Debbie doesn't remember Suzie's name, either, but I still knew Debbie was talking to me. The sad thing is, Debbie's not even gray yet. And she wouldn't belong in an old-folks' home, only Brookside isn't just for oldies.

It's for crazies.

Ma gets mad when I call them that, and everyone else working there would probably hate me if they heard me say it, because Brookside's motto is "Distinguished Memory Care." But that's just a fancy way of saying Crazy Town. The fact is, everyone living there has lost their mind. Or at least part of it. They can't remember stuff. Not from one day to the next and, for some of them, not from one minute to the next. There's one oldie named Stu who seems completely gone. He just sits in a corner and drools.

At least he's quiet. Debbie? Now, that's a different

story. I used to try and ignore Debbie, but it just made things worse. She got angry and kept asking the same question louder and louder until she was throwing stuff and screaming, "WHAT IS YOUR NAME?"

"It's not her fault," Ma told me. "Her brain's damaged. Just answer her straightaway and be done with it."

So when she shouted it this time, I called over, "It's Lincoln."

"Lincoln." She said it all breathless. Like I'd just given her a beautiful gift. "Abraham Lincoln was the sixteenth president of the United States, you know. My favorite."

That right there is a good example of why crazy is something I can't figure out. How can someone not remember your name after you've told it to them every single day for over a month but *can* remember that Abraham Lincoln was the sixteenth president?

I was relieved when Ma came out of one of the bedrooms and gave me her sweet smile. "Have a good day?" she asked.

Before I could even recall, Debbie turned to her and said, "Are you his mother?"

"I am," Ma answered, like it was a brand-new question instead of the same one she answered nearly every day.

Then Suzie York pointed at me and called out, "That boy knows how to get out of here!"

The crazies who'd been watching the action perked up a little, and the ones who were half asleep in their chairs sputtered awake and turned to stare at me.

Except for Droolin' Stu, who just sat there, drooling.

"He's just here to do his homework," Ma announced, and shooed me over to my table. Then she smiled around the room and asked, "Who wants a snack?"

Which was the end of anyone's interest in me.

9

Zombie Chicken

It was only four-thirty, but Teddy C had already forgotten about the snack and was demanding dinner. "Where's the food?" he hollered, pounding his fork and spoon on his table.

"It'll be here soon!" Gloria called as she helped another oldie to a table.

Dinnertime at Brookside is five o'clock. Two guys in hairnets roll it in on big metal carts from the kitchen. The oldies live for the carts, which hold the dinners and desserts for all thirty folks in the East Wing, and Ma says the exact same thing goes on in the West Wing.

Once the guys from the kitchen leave, the caregivers start handing around dinner plates while the nurses make sure the oldies who get meds take them.

The oldies sit four to a table, facing each other, saying nothing, unless it's "Where's the food?" It was creepy at first to see all these old folks looking like a bunch of zombies and then *eating* like a bunch of zombies, but Ma explained that they don't talk to each other because they're concentrating. "It's everything they've got just to get the food in," she told me. "Take a minute and really watch them, Lincoln. You'll see."

So I really watched them, and really watching them is not something I ever want to do again. It's *painful* to watch them eat. Their hands shake and they *focus* on putting food in, and then it takes years for them to swallow and start on the next bite.

There are usually the same four Purple Shirts in the Clubhouse during dinner. There's Ma, Gloria, and two others named Teena and Carmen. Teena's more no-nonsense with the oldies than Ma or Gloria, and Carmen's got a voice like gravel being shoveled. Teena and Carmen don't pay much attention to me, and I return the favor.

But back to oldies eating.

Gloria's the one who spends time spooning dinners into the oldies who are really bad off. Their dinners come blended, so what might have been chicken and rice and green beans to begin with winds up being three blobs of mush on a plate.

That's painful to watch, too, so I don't, which means I get a lot of homework done during dinnertime. Or, if I'm done with homework, I take out my notebook and work on my stories, which is the best way I know to block out what's going on around me.

After dinner, there are lots of leftovers. Not after dessert, but Ma says that some things stay the same no matter how old you get.

There's no Brookside dog, but if there was, he'd be big as a blimp on leftovers. Whole enchiladas and beef patties and chicken strips and biscuits . . . it's crazy what gets left on plates. And after dinner, *slop,* it all goes into the trash.

Ma has said more'n once what a waste it is, but who wants food that's been sitting at a zombie table? Especially since lots of times there's one little bite missing. Who's gonna eat that?

But the same day Kandi followed me, I saw Ma tuck away chicken strips in a plastic bag. Right there in front of God and the Purple Shirts, she slipped chicken and biscuits into a bag and put it in her purse.

Nobody said a thing, but I knew they were all thinkin' stuff, and I was sure embarrassed. It seemed so pitiful. No kidding Ma's tight with a dollar, but this I couldn't believe. And once I got over the shock of what she'd done, my mind started screamin' in terror.

She's gonna make me eat used food?!

On the bus ride home, she didn't say a word about it, so I finally asked, "Why'd you steal that chicken?"

She looked at me like I had holes for brains. "*Steal* it?"

"Okay, *take* it."

She studied me some more, then gave me a strange little look. Like someone at school might do if they were fixin' to give you a wedgie. "Maybe I'm tired of cooking," she said.

That did me in. "Ma!" I cried. "No! I ain't eatin' zombie chicken! I'll eat cereal, day and night! You never have to cook again!"

"Zombie chicken," she said with a look that made me sure my shorts would be up to my ears if we were standing. "And what did I tell you about 'ain't'?"

"You make me eat zombie chicken and 'ain'ts' are gonna slip out!"

"Hush," she said, 'cause folks on the bus were staring now, wonderin' what sort of ma made her boy eat zombie chicken.

After a bit she leaned sideways and whispered, "And you can relax. It ain't for you."

She gave me a devilish grin, which made my mind snap like a pea pod, scatterin' thoughts all around my head.

What was that grin about?

What was she *sayin'*?

And who was it for, then? We didn't have a dog, and we didn't know any, either.

Only one thought made any kind of sense. "No, Ma!" I told her, keeping my voice low. "I won't let *you* eat zombie chicken, either!"

She gave me a stern look. "There is nothing wrong with this chicken."

"Ma, no!"

She opened her purse a bit and sniffed. "Smells delicious, if you ask me."

"Ma, no!"

She closed her purse and heaved a sigh. "The problem here is that you've never been hungry."

"I've been hungry!"

She gave me another stern look. "I've seen to it that you have not."

"But—"

"Hush."

The bus squealed to a stop, and when the doors flapped open, Ma led the way out, saying good night to the driver and nudging me to do the same when I started down the steps without sayin' it.

We walked the two blocks home without talking. It was cold out, and dark, and the streets had that scary feel they get when the only folks left on them are the ones with no place to be. I was glad to get to our corner. Glad to see light pouring out of the market.

But instead of going up to our apartment, Ma told me, "Wait right here," and headed off without me.

"Ma!" I called, 'cause she'd never done that before, and I sure didn't want to be left on my own with street folks.

"Hush!" she said over her shoulder. Then she went up to a man sitting outside the market and handed him the zombie chicken.

He looked up at her real slow. Like one of the oldies at Brookside might have. Then he raised a hand to take the food and gave Ma a nod.

He'd been there every night since we moved in, and

we've seen Mr. Noe, the man who runs the market, shoo him away from the door with a broom when he's sweeping out the place. Mr. Noe doesn't say a word to him—he just swats at him with the broom like he's a big pile of dirt.

So sometimes the man sits near the front door, and sometimes he's up the sidewalk a ways by an old pay phone that's covered in graffiti. Wherever he sits, though, he always looks the same. He wears a grimy green beanie, an old blue jacket, and gloves with the fingertips ripped out. He sits on a worn wool blanket by a cardboard box with a sign that reads:

2 TOURS
NO HOME
ANYTHING HELPS

I used to think *anything helps* meant money.
Turns out it also means zombie chicken.

10

The Demon Feather

At my old school we had desks. They were ancient, but it didn't matter 'cause yours was *yours*. The top lifted up, you could stash all sorts of stuff in it, and nobody bothered you about the mess lurkin' inside. Unless a sandwich got rotten. Or a banana went past black and into gooey. Even then, it was no big deal. The teacher'd say, "Smells like it's time for a little desk cleanin'," and everyone would throw away their spoiled food and old papers and candy wrappers.

Lookin' back on it, those desks might have been old and creaky, but they were way better'n the ones we have at my new school. What I liked most about the old desks was knowing where the borders were. Borders were simple. Nobody ever hogged up part of your desk with their stuff, or edged you out when they got carried away with a project. If they got carried away, their stuff went *smack* onto the floor.

At Thornhill School, the desks may be new, but they're really just tables. Tables for two, with a wide-open shelf for each person that barely holds a thing. There's no border on the desktop between you and your partner, not even a drawn line. So it's hard to protect your territory 'cause stuff is always creeping across the table like it's on a stealth mission.

And if that's not bad enough, we have to sit with two tables shoved together, face to face, so there are four kids at one big, square table, with no borders.

A whole continent of desktops, with no borders.

When I asked Ms. Miller if it was going to be like this all year, she explained that sixth grade is "a time of community learning" and that "this is how things are done around here."

Ms. Miller has put all sorts of reminders about being part of the community on our classroom walls and even on the ceiling. Every possible inch is covered in bright colors invitin' us to get along. There's the Global Community part, with flags and maps and art from around the world. There's the United We Stand wall, with more maps and figures from U.S. history. And there's the Our Community wall, where our projects get posted around the Golden Rule display.

Maybe I wouldn't mind community learning if my

everyday community wasn't three girls with way too much stuff. I don't understand why they have to have ten of everything and, if they do, why can't they keep it in their own territory?

Rayne's got hair accessories that stack up as the day goes by. She usually comes to school with her hair clipped down or braided with ribbons or decorated somehow, but by the end of the day it's busted loose and in full mane mode, with her headbands and clips and ribbons or what-not roamin' wild across our continent.

Straight across from me, there's Wynne, and she goes through Kleenex like air. She breathes in, she sniffles out. "Sorry! Allergies," she whispered the first time I got fed up with her tissue avalanche and pushed it back on her side. "Sorry" hasn't stopped avalanches from happening, but I feel mean just shoving them back because she looks truly miserable with her nose drippin' and her eyes waterin'.

But the worst invader was Colby's pencil feather. It's pink and fluffy and has little fake jewels that kind of clink when she writes. Why does a pencil need a feather? And why does a feather need *jewels*?

That's accessories on accessories!

I wouldn't have cared, except Colby's feather made her pencil about two feet long, and since she sat right next to me, that feather would wag around in *my* airspace with its little fake jewels all clinkin' together.

Colby gets A's on everything, which Ma told me was a good reason to put up with her feather. But during tests, that feather flaps around like a demon bird, and what that *means* is, Colby's got answers.

Right off, my stomach would tie up in knots. How could she know the answers so fast? And how come all of a sudden I couldn't think of any?

All through September and all through October I forced myself to put up with Colby's demon feather. I would scoot to the side and try everything to ignore that feather flapping through the air.

Then November rolled around and Ms. Miller gave us a math test and none of my feather-fightin' tricks worked. I just couldn't concentrate. *Flap, flap, flap, flap, flap,* that demon feather went, whippin' through the air while Colby showed all her steps. It would glide for just a second as she put a box around her answer, then take off again, flappin' its way through the next problem.

I was so distracted that instead of working on the math test, my brain went off and made up a story. In it there was a big feather that released hypnotizing eraser dust that was used as a powerful weapon by an intergalactic queen named Colby. Queen Colby had hijacked the *Inquiry,* a spaceship that, until then, had been under the command of the famous Captain Jones. The feather had hypnotized the captain and he was now a desperate prisoner on his own ship.

There's a great battle in the story, where the captain finally defeats Queen Colby by snatching the feather and tickling her nose with it, bringing her down in a fit of sneezing. It was a pretty funny scene, and I was having a great time making it better and better in my head when Ms. Miller told us that test-taking time was up.

I saw her frown when she collected my paper, but I tried to duck out to recess anyway.

"Lincoln!" she called as I was bolting for the door.

"Yes, ma'am?"

"Stay in, please."

When the room was cleared of everyone but her and me, she held out my test and said, "Can you explain this?"

So I told her about Colby's demon feather.

"Why didn't you just ask her to use a different pencil?"

"I've asked her lots of times! She says it's her lucky feather."

"Couldn't you have turned away?" She shook her head. "What *did* you do the whole time?"

I didn't want to say "Nothing," so it slipped out about the story. And since I was nervous, more slipped out than I wanted.

"Lincoln," she said with a sigh. "Don't these sound like excuses to you?" The corners of her mouth twitched like they wanted to get up but were just too tired. "Do we need to talk to your parents about getting you a tutor?"

"No, ma'am! I know how to do this stuff."

Her mouth rolled over into a frown. "Lincoln."

"I swear, ma'am! It was the feather!"

"Fine," she said after studying me for a bit. "It was the feather." Then she sat me down at the table nearest her, put my test and a pencil in front of me, and said, "You've got until recess is over."

I never worked a math test so fast in my life. And when recess was done, so was I.

Ms. Miller took the test from me with an eyebrow stretched high, then checked it over quick with a red pen in her hand.

A red pen that only touched paper once.

She looked up at me, then wrote 96% and circled a big red A at the top. And when everyone was in from recess, she told Colby she couldn't use her demon feather pencil anymore.

"That's unconstitutional!" Colby cried, and she somehow twisted freedom of speech into freedom of feathers and got all uppity about her rights.

"Why don't I just switch seats with her?" Rayne asked, and once everyone was done being stunned by how nice it was for her to offer and what an easy fix it was, Rayne switched with Colby, putting that demon feather as far away from me as it could get on our borderless continent.

"Thanks," I told Rayne when she was all settled in.

"Sure," Rayne said, and gave me a smile that was one part twinkle and nine parts shy.

A smile that made my cheeks burn hot.

11

Talking in Circles

A strange thing happened after Rayne switched with Colby.

Kandi started stalking me.

She'd mostly left me alone after she'd followed me that day in early October. Oh, I'd see her giving me the spy-eye every now and then. My eyes hurt just seeing her do it, but maybe her eye muscles are looser than everyone else's. Maybe they're all limbered up from getting stretched around.

I don't really care that she does the spy-eye on me 'cause she seems to do it to everyone. I stuck out my tongue at her once when I caught her, but I felt stupid after, so now I just hit her with a straight-on stare, which makes her stop.

So Kandi hadn't said much to me for about a month,

but during lunch after the switch, she found me in the cafeteria and sat right across from me.

"Hi!" she said, sort of squiggling in her seat.

I kinda forgot to say hi back and just stared. I'm not used to talking to folks during lunch, especially not girls. I'm used to eating quick and getting over to the media center.

Kandi laughed. "What's the matter?"

I looked at my tray. "Uh . . . I'm almost done?"

She laughed again. "So? Just hang out and talk." She took a bite of her mac 'n' cheese. "How's your story coming?"

Her fingernails weren't painted like candy corn anymore. They were little turkeys with the tails all fanned out. "How do you do that?" I asked, 'cause the detail was crazy.

She put out a hand for me to admire. "You like?"

I was more *confused*. Or *puzzled*. Or maybe even *mystified*. Yeah, *mystified* fit the bill. "How long did that take you?" I asked.

She pulled back her hand. "You didn't answer my question."

I finished off my milk. "You didn't answer mine first."

"No, you didn't answer *mine* first."

I thought back and she was right. She'd asked me about my story. But the story about Annie and Howler was done, and I didn't want to waste time talking about my new story, I wanted to get back to *writing* it. I was at a heart-stopping spot where my main guy, Lucas, had barely escaped a killer by getting on the roof of a cabin. But the killer knew he was there and was climbing the side of the cabin by jabbing hunting knives into the wood as he went up, up, up. The wind was howling through the trees, so Lucas couldn't hear the killer coming.

That's where I'd had to stop. And since getting back to Lucas and the killer was something I wanted to do way more than talking in circles with Kandi, I stood up and told her, "Gotta go," and left.

I have a secret hideout in the media center. It's hidden by shelves of books in the far back corner, and above the shelves, clear up to the ceiling, the walls are painted with blue sky and clouds.

The librarian, Ms. Raven, goes crazy with decorations. Every inch of the walls is painted, and there are big cut-outs of characters standing around the place, and smaller ones hanging from the ceiling. There's the Reading Tree area, with a life-sized tree in the middle of a big cubby of picture books. I've seen little kids sitting around it on mats with books in their laps like they're havin' a picture-book picnic.

But back to my secret hideout.

It has a beanbag chair, soft as feathers, and that's what I sit in to write. Some lunches I wind up spending the time just staring at the painted sky and clouds, thinking about my story, but others I spend scribblin' the entire time.

My hideout's not actually *secret* as much as it is some-place no one else seems to go. Mostly, kids are at the computers. There are rows of them up front near Ms. Raven's desk, so that's where all the action is. Ms. Raven's nice, but what I like best is that she's quit askin' if she can help me. Now she just waves hello and lets me be.

And that's exactly what she did when I came in at lunch after ditching Kandi and her turkey-tail nails. Ms. Raven was over by the student stations, so I did a little double take when I passed by her desk 'cause there was a kid sitting at her computer.

There's no mistakin' whose computer it is 'cause there's an engraved brass plaque stating CARRIE C. RAVEN, LMS on it, and it has a big black bird perched on top.

I might've said something about him being back there, but Ms. Raven was lookin' right at us, so she already knew he was there. Then it clicked. "You her son?" I asked. It just came out.

"No!" he said. "She's helping me research."

The scowl on his face was tellin' me to move along—something I was more'n happy to do. I had a hero to save. A killer to stop. I needed to get Lucas off of that roof!

12

Invasion of Privacy

I didn't know I'd made Kandi mad until we were back in the classroom after lunch. Even then it took a little while to sink in because my mind was still on my story. I'd only had fifteen minutes in the beanbag chair, and the killer was now about to crest the roof while Lucas frantically looked for a way down.

"Did you hear me?" Kandi asked with a huff.

"Huh?" I asked back, 'cause I had no idea that she'd said anything.

"You were really mean to me," she said, and was she ever pouting!

"Uh . . . sorry. I didn't mean to be."

"Well, you were," she said, and stomped off.

Next to me, Rayne put a clip back in her hair and giggled.

I looked at her. "What?"

"She's not used to that."

"Used to what?"

Colby had her feather pencil out, ready for action. "Being ignored," she said without even looking at me.

Wynne leaned closer across our continent and whispered, "Can we pay you to keep doing it?" and the three of them giggled.

I didn't get it, but I also didn't care. It seemed like gossipy girl stuff to me. And then Ms. Miller started us on a timed write. *My favorite weather is . . .* , she wrote on the board, and like a switch going off, I forgot everything else and started writing.

When time was up, Kandi volunteered to collect the papers, and I could tell her eyes were slurping up words from the pages as she walked them up to Ms. Miller.

"She's reading yours," Rayne said, pulling the same hair clip back out.

"Who says it's mine?" I asked.

"Invasion of privacy," Colby called over her shoulder as she watched Kandi move toward Ms. Miller's desk.

Wynne was watching Kandi, too, and when she turned back around, she leaned forward and whispered, "You should complain."

"Who says it's mine?" I asked again, and this time they all answered me with looks that said I was dumber'n a load of bricks.

Which I guess I am, 'cause once again, I didn't hear Kandi

coming up behind me on my way to Brookside. Lucas was still on the rooftop in my mind, and I was trying to figure out how to get him down alive when she spooked me with "Don't you love this weather?"

I jumped. She laughed.

"Stop that!" I spat out.

"Why are you so skittery?"

"I'm not! I was just thinking!"

"About . . . ?"

"Look," I said, stopping dead in my tracks. "What do you want?"

"Nothing! I'm just in a great mood!" She gave me a big, sunny smile and said, "I think it's the weather. I just love the wind." She put her arms out and twirled around. "All that . . . energy!"

My jaw went for a dangle.

"What?" she asked.

"You read my paper."

"What are you talking about?" she asked, but guilt was stamped all over her face.

I gave her the stink-eye. "Don't lie!"

"Okay! So what if I read it?" she laughed. "It's not like it was personal." I was still giving her the stink-eye, so she said, "You're a good writer, Lincoln, you really are."

Then she twirled around and ran away.

13

The Vampire in Room 102

After Kandi followed me the second time, I kept a wary eye out for her and even took to going a longer way, just to throw her off my trail. I hid out from her at school, too, and after a while she started ignoring me back, which was a huge relief.

It took over two weeks, but finally one Friday it felt safe enough to take the shorter walk to Brookside, and I got there in time to see an ambulance parked by the main doors with its lights flashing and the engine running.

I hurried inside, but the East Wing and the West Wing were both closed, so I couldn't tell which side of the place the ambulance was for. I would have asked Geri when I signed in, but she was on the phone, recruitin' folks for the Alzheimer's Walk that was happening in early December.

Not that she would have told me much. She never does, unless the subject is the weather. But I would have asked anyway, especially since I've figured out that there's a vampire in Room 102.

Go ahead and laugh, but I'm not messing around. Room 102 has two beds. One of them's for Mrs. White—she's the vampire. The other's for somebody who has no idea they're about to die.

It's a sneaky situation, because Mrs. White doesn't *look* like a vampire. She actually looks like the one who's had all her blood drained. Her face is gray and bony, her hair is white and wispy, and her hands are one hundred percent knuckles.

She also *acts* dead. She just lies there, day after day, bony-faced and wispy-haired, asleep in her special motorized bed.

Ma explained to me that Mrs. White has a special bed because she's on hospice, which she also explained was a nice way of saying she's going to die. Very soon. Like, any day. Only Mrs. White hasn't died. Instead, she's outlived six roommates since Ma started working there.

Six!

Every one of those roommates was in *way* better shape than Mrs. White. They could get up and sit at a table for dinner. They could use a toilet and take a shower and go to the Activities Room, all while Mrs. White just lay there, looking dead.

One by one, though, the roommates suddenly died.

And every one of them died during the night.

And every time one died, Mrs. White bounced back to life.

"Just when you think *she's* the one who'll be gone by morning, she bounces back," Ma said after the third roommate, Cynthia, died back in early October. "I sat with her to distract her while they were clearing out Cynthia's things. Her cheeks were rosy. She smiled and talked . . . even thanked me after I changed her!"

We were on the bus ride home. And maybe it's 'cause we'd entered the month of ghouls and goblins, and spooky decorations were already up in store windows, but a funny idea about Mrs. White flashed into my brain. I kept my voice down as I broke the news to Ma. "That's because she's a vampire."

Ma gave me one of her looks. "Lincoln!"

I gave her one of *my* looks.

So she frowned at me and said, "That's the most ridiculous thing I've ever heard. She can't even get out of bed!"

"She doesn't need to," I whispered. "She's a *psychic* vampire."

"A *what*?"

"She sucks the life force out of folks," I told her.

"And how does she do *that*?"

I gave her a little grin. "You need to ask *her*."

I was just messing around, but less than two weeks later the next roommate mysteriously died during the night, and Ma kind of freaked out. "Mrs. White's cheeks were all rosy again!" she whispered on the bus ride home. "They haven't been rosy since the last time!"

"I told you," I said with a little shrug, "she's a psychic vampire." But this time I wasn't so sure I was messing around.

Then it happened *again*, and Ma really freaked out. "It's not funny!" she said. "It's the third one this month! It's like . . . it's like some sort of *hoodoo*."

The fifth roommate dying had caused Ma to work late, so it was darker'n usual as we were walking home from the bus stop. My eyes were dartin' around, taking in the creatures of the night hangin' out in doorways. "So don't go back in her room," I said, wondering how powerful a psychic vampire could get.

Ma drew her coat in tighter. "I have to! It's my job!"

I noticed the moon, shinin' near full above us. "Well, just don't go in her room after dark, then. And maybe wear some garlic."

"Garlic? Really?" she asked.

I pointed out the moon. "Couldn't hurt, right?"

I was expecting her to accuse me of having a wild imagination, but seein' the moon did her in. "Oh, Lord!" she gasped.

She tried to dial it back, telling me we were just over-reacting, but then she stopped at the corner market for some garlic. "Couldn't hurt, right?"

Ma seemed fine the next morning, but the instant I got to Brookside that afternoon, she hauled me into the

Clubhouse phone room and closed the door tight. "She noticed!" Ma gasped, and her eyes were wide as pies.

"Who noticed what?" I looked through the phone room window to see if anyone was watching, 'cause the room is small and being hauled into it felt mighty awkward.

"Mrs. White! She noticed the garlic!" Ma dropped her voice even more. "Her nose twitched! Like this," she said, then did a twitchy thing with her nose that made her look like a rabbit trying to sneeze. "And she asked, 'What *is* that foul odor?'"

I took a little step back 'cause Ma *was* smelling mighty garlicky. "Had she messed her diaper?"

"Yes! And she *still* noticed it! She acted like she was afraid of it!"

"Maybe she was talking about *her* smell?"

"She never talks about her smell, and her smell's a whole lot worse than garlic!"

"So . . . did you tell her?"

Her eyes about popped out. "That I was warding off her psychic vampire powers with garlic?!" She looked out the window to make sure no one had heard, 'cause it had come out so loud. But worse than someone hearing, the Brookside director, Mr. Freize, was entering the Clubhouse. "Oh, Lord," Ma gasped. She shoved me down in the phone chair. "Stay right here until I come get you. Look busy! Do your homework!"

"Ma, you should—"

"Hush!" she said, and hurried out of the room.

So I didn't get to tell her how garlicky she smelled.

I didn't get to tell her that she should steer clear of the director.

Too bad, too, 'cause she was all mortified on the ride home. "Did it really smell that strong?" she asked.

"Oh, yeah."

"I shouldn't have peeled them."

"You *peeled* them?"

"I didn't know! I've never had to ward off vampires before!"

"And *them*? How many did you have on you?"

"Never mind!" she snapped. Then she muttered, "They must've warmed up after I started working." She looked out the window. "It's not an easy job, you know."

We rode along for a while, quiet, until finally I asked, "You got rid of them, right?"

"Of course I got rid of them!"

She wasn't in the mood to hear it, but I felt like I needed to tell her. "It still smells, Ma."

That night she took a shower until the hot water was all gone. And the next day Mrs. White had a brand-new roommate, named Mary. "She's sweet and gentle, and her daughter seems so nice," Ma told me with tears in her eyes.

Sure enough, near the end of her second week, Sweet Mary died unexpectedly during the night. November was starting off the same way October had, and I couldn't help wondering again how powerful a psychic vampire could

get. Especially with the nights getting longer. Did it give her more time to use her powers? Would she be reaching through walls soon?

"Go in there and look!" Ma said, pointing at Mrs. White's room. "Her cheeks are all rosy. She's *giggling* and wanting to go for a walk!"

"I'm not going in there!" I told her, and made a beeline for my table.

Mrs. White didn't actually get up and go for a walk that afternoon. She just lay in her special bed while they finished cleaning out Mary's half of the room.

About two weeks had passed since Mary died, so I figured the ambulance idling in front of Brookside had something to do with Mrs. White killing off her new roommate—a big, boxy woman named Pat.

The truth is, I was more worried about Ma being freaked out than I was about Pat being dead, but when the East Wing door opened, I quit worrying about either. It w Debbie Rucker who was being wheeled out, and she as alive as ever.

Geri was still on the phone, so I hurried over the door.

"What is your name?" Debbie demanded saw me.

"Lincoln," I told her.

"Well, Lincoln, guess what?" she said and I have to go to the hospital!"

"Hope you're okay," I said.

"I'll be fine!" she told me. Then in a big burst she called, "Lincoln was the sixteenth president! My favorite!"

I caught the East Wing door before it latched.

"Don't let them throw out my snack," Debbie hollered over her shoulder. "Did you hear me, Lincoln? Don't let them throw out my snack!"

I pushed the door open. All of a sudden I was ready for a snack. Maybe two!

I lost my appetite quick, though, 'cause that was the same day Ruby Hobbs begged Gloria to let her dance.

It hit me hard. I'd been spendin' my afters at Brookside for over two months and sure hadn't seen it coming, but somewhere along the line the oldies had become *people* to me. People with feelings. So as tough as it was for my eyes to take, seein' Ruby the way she was didn't seem so funny anymore.

14

Messengers

It took a lot of *there, theres* and *now, nows* from Gloria to get Ruby to stop crying and back in her room. When Ruby came out for supper a bit later, she was dressed and quiet, but in some ways her being quiet was even sadder than her crying, 'cause she just sat at the table looking down. It was like she was too tired to eat. Too tired to care.

"Why does she do that?" I asked Ma on the way home.

"Do what?" Ma whispered, looking around the bus. "And who are we talking about?"

"Ruby," I said. "Why does she come out all buck naked, singing?"

"Oh," Ma said, heaving a sigh. "I'm sorry you had to see that."

"It's the third time I've seen it!"

"I'm up to about ten."

"But why does she do it?"

Ma shook her head. "I don't know." Then she gave a little shrug and said, "Why do any of them do what they do? Like Peggy Riggs. Why does she talk to the air?"

Peggy Riggs did talk to the air. And she did it like the air was listening. Like she was sharing secrets with someone she could see. Only the secrets didn't make any sense.

"Maybe she's seeing ghosts?" I said. "There's got to be *lots* of ghosts in that place. Especially with Mrs. White on the loose at night."

"Lincoln, hush. I am just too tired to have you piling ghosts on top of vampires." She sank down in her seat a little, hugging her bag. "It was a mighty long day."

Ma turned to look out the window, so my mind wandered off. And it probably would've got totally lost if Ma hadn't snapped me back a short while later. "Huh?" I asked, 'cause she was staring at me and I knew she'd said something.

"Where do you go when your eyes get like that?" she asked.

"Get like what? What are you talking about?"

"They move around like you're watching something."

"They do?"

"Mm-hmm. So what were you thinking just now?"

I did some blinking as I remembered, then finally told her, "You don't want to know."

She gave me the same look she does when I'm about to get it for sassin'. "Yes, Lincoln. Yes, I do."

I was pretty tired, too, and sure didn't need trouble piled on top of tired. "I was just thinkin' . . . ," I said, but something told me to stop.

"Don't make me drag it out of you, boy. Just say it!"

"All right, all right!" I took a breath and started, "You know how Crazy Paula does that tapping thing?"

"Paula *Barnett*? At Brookside? You're thinking about *her*?" Then real quick she added, "And don't call her crazy."

I stared at her. "Ma, if there's such a thing as crazy, she's it."

She frowned. "You could call her Tapping Paula."

"That's worse! No one hates her for being crazy. They hate her for tapping."

Which was a fact so solid, Ma couldn't argue. Paula sits day after day, with eyes drooped to half-mast, doing nothing, then one hand starts tapping on the table, over and over and over and over, until you want to scream, *Stop it!*

"That tapping really gets to me," Ma said, twisting around to look at me. "Why does she do it? Why won't she stop?"

"*That's* what I was thinkin' about," I told her. And once that busted out, the rest started flowing. "Maybe she can't speak, but what if she can see things we can't?"

Ma sat back again and heaved another sigh. "What *are* you talking about?"

I knew she was tired. Tired and testy. I knew I should probably make up something else and not tell her what I was really thinking. But I'd had this *idea*. I could see the whole thing! "What if she can see ghosts?" I asked, lettin' more seep out. "What if they can tell her things?" Ma's eyes rolled, but I kept talking. "Paula's on the border, right? Of here and there? Of earth and after? She's got to be, right?"

Ma's whole head turned now, and she just stared at me. And I knew I should just hush up, but it was too late. I had that feeling I get when everything comes together in one picture that's big and clear and bright and . . . *amazing.*

So it gushed out. "What if all that tapping Paula does is a way of *communicating?* Like Morse code? Everyone *thinks* she's crazy, but maybe she's not! Maybe she's tryin' to tell the ghosts something! Or maybe she's tryin' to tell *us* something! Like that Mrs. White is about to strike again!"

The words hung there, hovering in the dim light inside the bus. And I had to admit—the idea had seemed way better bouncing around inside my head than it did running out my mouth.

Ma closed her eyes and took a deep breath. "Lincoln Jones, you have an imagination as wide as it is deep."

And then *that* just hung there, actin' like a compliment, when I'm pretty sure it wasn't.

At our stop, Ma gave me a little scowl as she gathered her stuff. "One thing's for sure," she said. "I'm not taking your advice about dealing with the residents. I'm done with vampires and ghosts and Morse-coding mutes."

Couldn't blame her there.

The wind blasted cold and sharp when we got off the bus, and we hunkered in against it as we walked home, me half a pace behind her. Neither of us said a word until we were almost to our corner, where Ma suddenly stopped short. "I forgot the Man's dinner," she said, then shook her head and started walking again. "It's sittin' right in the fridge."

Ever since I'd told Gloria what Ma was up to with her taking home zombie chicken, word had gotten around Brookside, and now the others helped Ma pack a dinner for "the Man."

"Sweet of you, Maribelle," they all said, but I suspect most of them thought *I* was "the Man."

As we walked along, Ma kept kicking herself for forgetting. I tried telling her to go easy on herself, but when the Man saw us coming, it was like a light went on in his eyes.

"Oh, Lord," Ma said under her breath.

And then, to make things worse, he did something he'd never done before.

He stood up.

"Lord, oh, *Lord*," Ma whimpered.

"It's okay," I told her, but it was just words, and I knew it.

"I'm sorry," she said, going up to him. "I don't have anything today."

But he wasn't looking for food. "Is your name Maribelle?" he asked.

Ma's face went a little loose.

I guess the Man knew how to read loose faces, 'cause he pointed to the pay phone and said, "You had a call. Your sister. She wants you to call her back."

"Oh, Lord," Ma said, then recovered with a polite nod. "Well, thank you very much."

"It kept ringing and ringing," the Man said, shaking his head. "At first I didn't know what it was. It never rings."

"I appreciate the message," Ma said with another nod. "Sorry if it disturbed you."

"Disturbed me?" He gave her a strange little smile. "It was no trouble."

"Well, thank you," Ma said.

When she started to leave, he said, "I'm Levi, by the way."

Then he sat back down and looked away.

15

Hide 'n' Seek

Ma handed me her key and said, "I've got to call Ellie. Go warm the stew. I'll be right up."

"But—"

"Git!"

She zapped me hard with the steely-eye, and since there's no arguing with Ma's steely-eye or her *git*, I got. But I was burning with questions! Why had Ma given Aunt Ellie the pay phone number? We didn't have a phone, but why not give Aunt Ellie the number at Brookside, like she'd done for the school when she'd filled out my forms? And why was Aunt Ellie calling, relaying messages through street folk? What was so important? It couldn't have anything to do with Ma not repaying her. Everything we did—or, more like, *didn't* do—seemed to come back to us still owing Aunt Ellie. Every time Ma got paid, she sent Aunt Ellie money, and every time I asked for something, I got told, "Not until I've got Ellie paid back." Even Snickers bars got nixed.

All this went sparking through my brain at light speed. And since Ma's steely-eye wasn't glaring at me right then, I had a full recharge of curiosity, which got me doin' an about-face back to the gate.

I opened the gate as quiet as I could, and spy-eyed the corner. I could see Ma hunkered against the phone with her back to me, so I went through the gate and edged in closer.

What I heard set my heart scampering like a rabbit. "He won't, Ellie," Ma was saying. "He can't even get himself to work. How's he ever going to get it together to track me down?" She listened for a bit, then said, "I'm sure he was! That's how he gets when he's drinking." She added the *g* at the last minute. Like she was remembering how to speak a foreign language. Then she heaved a sigh and said, "Look, if it happens again, just keep denying you've seen us. . . . Yes . . . Yes . . . I know. . . . Yes'm. And you know I appreciate it. . . . I will. And I'll put some extra in the last one. You should have it before Christmas. . . . Mm-hmm . . . I'm sorry about the trouble. Really, I am."

I should've backed away the second I knew Aunt Ellie had called about Cliff, but I got greedy, wanting to know more, and gettin' greedy always bites me in the backside.

"Lincoln!" Ma snapped when she saw me trying to steal

away. She came steaming at me like a locomotive. "Since when do you flat out disobey me?"

"Since the stairs are dark and I got scared?" I gave her my best pleading look. "You never let me go up or down by myself after dark!"

It was enough to not get me cuffed, though I'm pretty sure she knew I was playing hide 'n' seek with the truth.

She snatched the key back from me and said, "What did you hear?"

"That Cliff's after us."

"He ain't *after* us!" she said, spitting the words out hard and fast.

When Ma's not clownin' around, "ain't" means she's simmerin' in stress. And since this time the word popped out like a bubble breaking through heatin' stew, I knew it was bad.

"Sorry," she said, calming herself as she went through the gate and closed it behind us. "I don't want you to worry. He will never in a million years come out here."

As we headed up the steps, I told her, "We need to get a phone, Ma. We need to get a phone so we can call 911 if he does show up."

"It's a mighty big world, Lincoln. And he's about as enterprisin' as a barstool. Look how long it's taken him to lift his dialin' finger—we've been gone since July! Besides, no one but Ellie knows we're out here, and she doesn't know where we're livin' or where I'm workin'."

"Is that why you didn't tell her? Because you were afraid Cliff would track us down?"

"He's never gonna track us down. Not with us this far away. I'm guessin' he's finally been evicted, which is why he's callin' around now. He's at a dead end with me, so his next move'll be to sweet-talk his way into some other woman's home, Heaven help her." She locked me down with double-barreled eyeballs. "We've got nothin' to worry about, you hear?"

"Then why didn't you tell Aunt Ellie our address or where you work?"

"Maybe I didn't want her weighin' in on where we live or what I do." She shook her head. "Lord, she would have *so* much to say!"

It still didn't make sense. "But why give her the pay phone number? We can't hear it ring."

She frowned. "I didn't give her the number. She got nosy and wrote it down from caller ID when I called once before about sending her payments." She frowned even harder. "And now she's all wantin' to know who 'my man' is."

"You mean Levi?"

She flashed a look at me. "I am tryin' to *forget* his name."

"But why, Ma?"

"Because now he's not just a man." She pulled out her key and slid it in the lock. "Now he's *somebody*. Somebody's son. Or brother. Or father. Maybe all three!"

I hurried to follow her inside. "But . . . wasn't he always?"

She clicked on a lamp, then turned to face me. "Somebody named him, Lincoln. The same way I named you."

I didn't like the way that felt.

Not one bit.

So I switched back to Aunt Ellie. "Well? What did you tell her?"

"Who? Ellie? I told her the truth."

"That he's a homeless guy?"

"No! That it's a pay phone."

When she set her bag down on the kitchen table, it seemed to pull her heart down with it. "It's gonna be okay, Ma," I said, touching her arm.

The words floated around us, feeling strange.

Like I was still playing hide 'n' seek with the truth.

16

Footsteps

After the business with Aunt Ellie and the pay phone, Ma seemed to be carrying the world on her shoulders, so I got to heating what was left of the stew like she'd asked me to do before she'd caught me spying.

Ma's stew's a wonder. It starts on Sunday and usually lasts to Friday, and along the way it shrinks and grows and changes flavor. She messes with it some nights, adding spices and chopping in more stuff. I like when she goes heavy on the carrots. Something about carrots stewing in beef juices and onions makes me happy to be hungry.

It didn't take long to heat, and when I had two steaming bowls with buttered bread on the table, Ma gave me a grateful smile and we both dug in.

Most days, Ma gets me talking about school over dinner, but not this time. Two bites in, her whole face seemed to crumple and sag as she scooped up stew. Every time she slid the spoon back in, it was slow and careful, like she was looking for answers between the onions and carrots.

It wasn't until her spoon was clinking the bottom that she finally said something.

"What?" I asked, because it was more mutter than words.

She looked up like she'd forgotten I was there, then ditched the brooding and went straight to huffy. "You'd think she could have invited us to Thanksgiving."

"Aunt Ellie?" I asked, running to jump onto her train of thought.

"Of course Ellie," she snapped.

My eyebrows couldn't help creepin' up. "You told me you were working a long shift on Thanksgiving. You said there was no gettin' out of it."

"Ellie doesn't know that!"

"But . . . if she'd asked us to dinner, you'd have had to tell her no, right?"

"She didn't even bother to ask!"

I wrestled with that, trying to figure out how a person could be mad over not being asked to do something they knew they couldn't do in the first place. And after flipping it back and forth in my mind for a while, I said, "What if she was waitin' for *you* to ask?"

"We can't have Thanksgiving here! We don't even have an oven!"

"But . . . she doesn't know that, right?"

"Lincoln! Whose side are you on?"

I went back to my stew. Maybe it *was* a better place to find answers. "Didn't know there was sides," I grumbled.

She held her forehead like it was all of a sudden too heavy to hold itself up. Then she sighed and said, "I never should have asked her for help."

"But . . . if you hadn't asked her for help, we'd still be—"

"Stop, Lincoln! Just stop!" She kicked back from the table and snatched up her bowl. "I will never hear the end of Cliff 'striking terror' in her heart." She zoomed in on me and snatched up my bowl. "I can't pay that off, you understand?"

My stomach was set on having seconds, so I was about to grab for my bowl, but suddenly Ma went all pie-eyed.

"What?" I asked, 'cause she looked like some freeze-frame out of a horror movie.

And then I heard them, too.

Footsteps.

In the whole time we'd lived there, no one had gone in or out of the apartment down the hallway. There was no noise through the wall, either. I wasn't even sure it *was* an apartment next door, seeing how there was no window along the walkway like ours had. "I think it's just a storage room," I told Ma after we'd been living there a couple of weeks.

"So why's there a *B* on the door and a *B* on the mailbox next to ours?" she asked.

Which was true, only the *B* mailbox never seemed to have anything in it.

"I bet it's condemned," she said a few days later when she noticed how our floor sags by the wall we share with *B*. And after inspecting it some more, she told me, "Don't walk over here, you hear me, Lincoln? It'd kill me if you crashed to your death before I could get us in a better place."

I tested the floor myself after she'd gone to bed, and it was springy all right, but nothing that was gonna swallow me whole. Besides, the market was straight below. If I crashed through after hours, there'd be Snickers to keep my mind off the pain.

But back to the footsteps.

Since nobody ever came up the stairs and nobody ever came to our door, hearing steps outside on any other day would have been strange, but now?

Visions of Cliff popped into my head.

"Who's out there?" Ma whispered.

Like I could tell with the blinds shut?

"Switch off the light!" she told me, scurrying to put the bowls down.

"Why?"

"Just do it!" she hissed.

So I did, and after we stood around in the dark for a minute listening and hearing nothing, Ma crept over to the window, put two fingers between blind slats, and spread them apart slow and sly.

"Is it Levi?" I whispered, hoping it was the Man and not Cliff.

"Hush," she said, like she was stifling a sneeze. Then she spread the slats wider and looked down toward B.

"Is it Cliff?"

She interrupted her spying to look at me like I was dumber'n dirt. "What did we just talk about? And how on earth could it be him?"

"So who, then?"

She went back to spying through the blinds. "It would help if there was a light out there. And I don't hear anything anymore!"

I tried getting in to see, but she swatted me away. And then, like rolling thunder, those footsteps were back.

Ma jumped away from the window and sucked in a scared breath.

"Who is it?" I asked. "Did you see?"

Before she could say, our door went *bam, bam, bam,* and you'd better believe I jumped back, too.

"Hello?" a man's voice called. "I've got a delivery for next door. Can you help me out?"

"A delivery?" I whispered, exchanging pie-eyes with Ma.

"Please," the voice said. "I'm from Shop-Wise Grocers, just trying to make a delivery. My truck broke down, which is why I'm so late. I think Mrs. Graves is already asleep."

Ma did squinty-eyes at me and mouthed, *"Who?"*

She'd moved aside, which gave me a clear shot at the window. So I darted over and peeked through the blinds.

There was a man out there, but it wasn't Cliff fakin' a delivery. Or Levi the Zombie Chicken Man.

It was . . . a leprechaun.

That's what he looked like, anyway. He was short with kinda pointy ears and was wearing big boots and a green Shop-Wise ball cap. There were tufts of red hair poking out around the cap and his ears, and his stomach was like a little potbellied stove, pushing out against his Shop-Wise shirt.

"Ma!" I said, ditching the blinds and shooting her a frown. "What are you 'fraid of?" Then I switched on the light and yanked open the door.

"Oh, *thank you*," Leprechaun Man said with a mighty gust of air. "It's been a horrible day." He set two bags of groceries inside and handed Ma a clipboard. "If you could sign right here?"

Ma didn't take the clipboard. "I'm afraid you've got the wrong place."

"Don't I wish. But no, I've been here every other week for years." He smiled, and his teeth were like shiny stars flashing through deep space. "But *you're* new."

Ma just stared at him.

The stars went dark, and he heaved a sigh. "Please. If you could just give these bags to her in the morning? She's my last stop. I'd really like to get home."

"Who's your last stop?" Ma asked.

"Carol Graves? Your neighbor in *B*?"

Ma looked down the hallway. "Someone's *living* there?"

I could see a whole litter of thoughts go scampering through his mind. But all he said was, "Yes. And you'd be doing us both a big favor."

I reached for the clipboard, but Ma snatched it first. "You're signin' nothing," she growled at me, then scribbled something that was definitely not her signature and handed the clipboard back.

"Thanks," Leprechaun Man said, and he was gone before the ink was done drying.

"So now what?" I asked Ma when the door was closed.

She frowned, first at the bags, then at me. Like it was *my* fault there were strange groceries in the room.

"Check for perishables," she said, turning her frown back to the bags.

"For church food?" I asked, 'cause I didn't know what *perishable* meant and that was the first thing that popped into my head.

"*Perish*," she said, "not *parish*."

Sounded pretty much the same to me.

"Stuff that might spoil," she added, nosing through the first bag like a twitchy little mouse. "That's what the ladies at Brookside call it."

When she'd moved on to the second bag, I couldn't keep it in anymore. "Any Lucky Charms?"

She stopped nosing. "Lucky Charms?" She frowned at me. "Even if there was, I wouldn't let you at them. This food is not ours."

"No! I meant because . . ." I shook my head. "Never mind."

"There's cans of soup," she said, moving on. "And apple-sauce . . . and oatmeal . . . a bottle of cranberry juice . . . and cat food."

"There's a *cat* living next door?" I asked, caught up in the wonder of it. I'd never heard mewing or scratching or . . . anything. But right through the saggy-floor wall was a cat?

"And a person," Ma said, and she seemed to be caught up in the wonder of that, too.

17

The Silver Cat

Cats like me. I don't know why, but they do. Back in my old neighborhood they'd follow me, slinkin' along ten yards behind me like little spies. I'd coax them in with empty tuna cans and then sit and stroke them over and over and over. Something about the flick of their tails. And their fur, so soft and smooth. And the way they nuzzle in for a rub when they're done scouring tuna. Yes, sir. Me and cats get along fine.

Ma said she was beat-up tired from her long week at Brookside and went to bed early. I was so happy to not be at Brookside or school that I sure didn't want to waste free time sleeping. Besides, I needed to get back to my story. Lucas was still on the roof with a killer after him, and I couldn't just leave him there. How was he going to escape?

The killer was determined! And could fling a knife with the speed and aim of an arrow!

So I got back to writing and followed Lucas to a point where he was considerin' leaping from the roof to escape the killer. He couldn't go down the way he'd come up—that's where the killer was! But jumping would be mighty painful. It was a long way down, and if he broke bones, he'd be crumpled and crippled—a sitting duck! The killer would laugh at him—*bwa-ha-ha*—from the rooftop, then send the wicked point of a knife flying straight through his heart.

Jumping seemed the only choice, but just as Lucas was fixin' to do it, a cat appeared on the rooftop. It was a silver cat, silent as snow, with emerald eyes and abalone claws, and it ran straight for the killer, whose head had just appeared over the roofline.

The cat hissed at the villain, its mouth wide and fierce.

"Nice kitty, good kitty," the killer said as he yanked a knife from the side of the cabin. But before the villain could strike, lightning claws slashed across his face. "Aaargh!" he cried, and then down, down, down he fell.

"Well, hey there," Lucas said, crouching beside the cat. And as they both looked over the edge at the crumpled killer below, he added, "Thank you."

"Mrow," the cat said back, then nuzzled Lucas's leg, finding the pocket where a tuna sandwich had been a few hours before.

The story wrapped up great after that, and even though

it was really late when I finally wrote *The End*, I wasn't tired. I was too happy to be tired. The bad guy was defeated! And I really liked the cat. I even changed the name of the story to "The Silver Cat," and I started thinking maybe I'd write more stories about him. There was something cool and mysterious about him. Pretty soon I started imagining what it would be like if the Silver Cat had some sort of telepathy.

What if he could read Lucas's mind?

I fell asleep thinking about the Silver Cat. And when the smell and sizzle of sausages cooking woke me up, it was from a dream about the Silver Cat. I don't remember much about it except for purring. That was enough, though. The Silver Cat was happy being in my dream.

Ma seemed recharged, even hummin' a little as she fixed breakfast. And I was all for her being in a good mood. There's nothing like grits *and* eggs *and* sausage to start a day off right.

"Thanks, Ma," I told her after I was stuffed to the gills.

She smiled at me and said, "I have a hunch you're gonna need the fortification."

Sounded like trouble to me. "What are you talkin' about?"

"Carol Graves. Our neighbor."

"Why does having a neighbor take fortification? What does that even mean?"

"It means you'll be needing your strength."

"Uh . . . why?"

"Because I've been thinking," she said, clearing plates.

"Uh-oh," I said under my breath.

"We've been living here nearly three months, and the whole time we've had no idea she was in there. Who's taking out the garbage? Who's doin' the laundry? Who's cleaning the cat box?"

"Not me!" I said, twisting around in my chair.

"My guess is she's old."

"Old?" Nowhere on my wish list was getting to know another old person.

"Applesauce, oatmeal, cranberry juice, soups . . . nothing solid. I'm guessin' she's old, has trouble with her teeth, and could probably use a little help."

"Ma, no! Don't we help enough old folks every single day?"

"We?" She gave me the steely-eye. "And it's not every single day."

"But today's *Saturday*. Can't we get away from old folks on our one day off?"

"Lincoln," she warned. "I don't know what the situation next door is, but you're coming with me, and if some trash needs taking out, you're volunteerin' to do it." She frowned. "And right now, I'd like you to volunteer to do the dishes."

I didn't say what I was thinking—that volunteering was not the same as being ordered around. I just frowned right back and said, "Yes, ma'am."

But while I was doing the dishes, I started wondering

if the cat next door was silver. And if its eyes were green. And if it had claws like abalone shells.

Maybe that's why the Silver Cat had popped into my story. Maybe he *did* have telepathy!

I got so deep into picturing the cat and how it was going to purr, and feel so soft, and maybe read my mind, that by the time Ma was ready to go, I was all for taking out the neighbor's trash.

"Here," Ma said, handing me a Shop-Wise grocery bag. "You take one, I'll take the other. That way it'll seem like we're both there for a reason, not just nosing into her business."

It seemed a surprising thing for her to say. "So we're going over to nose into her business?"

Ma eyed me. "I'm pretty sure her business needs some nosing."

"But nobody wants their business nosed into. I sure don't want her nosing into ours!"

"Well, hers needs it. Ours doesn't."

"But . . . how do you know?"

"Oh, hush, Lincoln," she said, closing our door and leading me down the hallway. "Just trust me."

18

The Dangling *B*

There's no such thing as doorbells in our building, so Ma just went right up and rapped on the door with the dangling *B*.

Ma's got solid knuckles. Knuckles that mean business. Still, no one came runnin' to answer the door. She waited a minute, her ear perked near the flaky paint of the door, before using those knuckles again. "Mrs. Graves!" she shouted. "We've got your groceries!"

After another minute, I whispered, "I still say it's just storage. Or empty. Look at the knob." It was loose from the wood, and kind of sloppy. Like nothing important was stored behind it, and definitely not a person.

Which made me think that the Shop-Wise guy was actually just a wise guy who'd played some sort of trick on us. Although I couldn't really put my finger on what that trick might be.

Ma's mind wasn't on storage *or* the Shop-Wise guy. "Ha!" she huffed, giving me the sly-eye, with a grin to match. "Here she comes." She pulled her ear away from the door and whispered, "A hundred dollars says she's old."

I had all of zero dollars, so I couldn't take that bet. And that's a good thing, 'cause when the door finally creaked open, we were definitely looking at old.

Old face.

Old clothes.

Old *smell.*

"Mrs. Graves?" Ma asked, turning up the volume. "We're your new neighbors. I'm Maribelle, and this is my son, Lincoln."

She said it like she was talking to someone underwater, but the words still seemed to swim right by Mrs. Graves.

"We have your groceries!" Ma shouted.

"I can hear you, Maribelle," the old lady said, and she bared her dingy teeth a little, like a dog fixin' to bite. Then she turned to me and said, "Nice to meet you, Lincoln," and did the dog-bite thing again, which I was catching on was her way of smiling.

Ma held her bag a little higher. "Would you like us to carry these into your kitchen?"

"Not necessary," Mrs. Graves said back.

"We don't mind," Ma said. "And Lincoln would be happy to take out your trash, or whatever else needs doing."

Mrs. Graves gave me a doubtful look. "He would, would he?"

"Sure," I said after Ma nudged me. And it did seem like something I should do. Besides being old, Mrs. Graves was small. Her body was like twigs stuck together inside a heavy wool sweater.

I sneaked a peek past her, wondering how much work I might have gotten myself into. Her place was bigger than ours, but what I noticed most was sunshine. It's something that never sets foot in our place, but here, right next door, it streaked in through a window, making the air seem like it was dusted with gold.

A cat nosed in, its face poking out between the door and Mrs. Graves's leg. It was black and white and had crazy green eyes that were bright and deep and hypnotizing.

"Me-ow!" it cried, and the sound was so pitiful I had an instant wish for a can of tuna.

I knelt down to pet it and could see another cat padding over that looked like the twin of the first cat, but wasn't. It was the mirror image. All the markings were in the exact opposite place, except the white tip of the tail, which was in the exact *same* place.

I was so busy figuring out the Mirror Cats that at first I didn't see a third cat coming from the other side of the room. It was dusty gray and small, with one eye insistin' on sleeping while the other one was wide open, scouting things out. I thought, *Pretty neat trick,* but as the cat moved closer, I figured out that the one eye wasn't sleeping after all. It was missing.

My mind started flashing around. Whatever had happened must've been epic. Maybe dogs had cornered him in a dark alley! Maybe he'd been viciously attacked! Left for dead with a geyser of blood spurting from his eye!

I was just picturing him staggering home in a tattered war uniform, with a crutch and a lame leg to go along with his bloody eye, when Mrs. Graves pushed One Eye aside with her foot.

It was a quick move, and she did the same thing to the other two without even looking down. "Just leave the bags there," she told Ma, pointing to the ground at our feet.

"They're heavy," Ma said. "Why don't you let us—" But the door was already closing in Ma's face.

After staring at flaky paint for a solid minute, Ma finally set her bag down next to where mine was already resting. "Did you see the cats?" I whispered on our way home, and I was all pumped up.

"I didn't have to see them to *smell* them," she said, letting us into our apartment. "How can she even breathe in there?" Her head quivered like the tail of a snake, and what rattled out of her mouth was, "Where are her kids? Where is her family? What is *wrong* with folks?"

"What do you mean?"

"Didn't you notice? There were dishes everywhere! And piles of garbage!"

I almost let out, "There were?" but I pulled back the reins in time and said, "Maybe she doesn't have kids?"

"I saw pictures. In frames. By her couch."

"You *did*?"

"I've got a good eye for these things," she said, giving me a stealthy look.

I couldn't believe how we'd been looking through the exact same doorway and had seen such different things. "Were they pictures of *people*?" I asked.

"What else would they be of?"

"I don't know . . . cats?"

She grinned at me like she thought I was joking, but when she saw I wasn't, she got all serious. "Her kids need to know."

"Need to know what?"

"That she's living in unsanitary conditions with seventeen cats!"

"*Seventeen?* I only saw three!"

"Where there's three, there's seventeen," she said with a huff.

That made no kind of sense to me, but she sure seemed serious.

And I liked the happy feeling that it might be true.

19

The Laundromat

Saturday is Ma's one full day off, but she treats it like a workday, which means it's a workday for me, too. Groceries. Laundry. Cooking. Cleaning. It's a full day of gearing up for the next week, and the only part of it that feels like any kind of time off is being at the Laundromat.

I like the Laundromat. I like the way it smells, the way it sounds, the way it's noisy and quiet and busy and still all at the same time.

The folks who use it are interesting, too. They're fun to watch because you can tell they've got *stories,* which I try to piece together from the way they act and the things they say and do.

What kind of ruins the Laundromat for me, though, is Ma. She'll fidget and frown and flip through one aban-

doned magazine after another without reading much of anything. Once in a while she'll get up to check the machines to see how much longer it's gonna be.

"Wish *I* had a good book," she'll grumble when she goes past me. Or, worse, she'll nose in and say, "What *are* you writing?" when I'm scribbling fast on a story.

One time I sat a bit away from her and tried to pretend she was a stranger, just to see what story I might put together from watching her. I couldn't get past *knowing* her, though, and then she went and slapped down her magazine and said, "What *are* you doing?"

I guess my spy-eye wasn't being too sly.

I've also tried a bunch of times to get her to go do the other errands and let me watch the clothes, but she always does a leery-eye around the place and whispers, "I'm not leaving you with derelicts and drifters, Lincoln."

I tell her, "They're just doin' their laundry," but what I always get back is a highfalutin "Mm-hmm" and a look that says my mind's turned to mud.

The day we got shut out by Mrs. Graves and her cats, though, Ma seemed different at the Laundromat. She wasn't flipping through magazines or pacing around. She was just sitting there, staring off into space.

"What, Ma?" I finally asked, 'cause her being so still was making it hard to concentrate on my new story, which was about a hunched old lady who magically transformed into a fierce and awesome ninja cat at night. Or maybe she was fierce and *evil*; it was too soon to tell.

But back to Ma.

I had to ask her, "Ma?" again and give her a little shake before she turned to me and said, "What? Oh." And then her face started doing this witchy-twitchy thing like she was either about to cry or trying to cast some sort of spell on me.

"Ma!"

The witchy-twitchy thing stopped. "How old are you?"

You better believe that sent worry shooting straight through me. Was working with old folks all day making her lose her mind?

Was crazy *contagious*?

"Ma!"

She swiped a hand in front of her face like she was erasing one thought and starting over with another. "What I mean is, are you going to remember all this?" She looked around the Laundromat. "How's it going to settle in your mind?"

Her eyes were going all glassy, but I couldn't figure out why. "What are you *talking* about?"

She turned her glassy eyes on me. "Are you going to look back and hate me?"

"Hate you? Why would I hate you?"

She shook her head. "I'm trying, Lincoln. Really, I'm trying."

"I know that!"

She looked down at her hands. And after a long, quiet spell she said, "My life started going bad at eleven. It

was almost surely goin' bad before then, but I remember eleven being when I really started feelin' it. Eleven's when I started to *see* things."

"Like what?"

"Like about my ma and the way she . . . the way she wasn't there for us." She shook her head. "And Lord, did I resent Ellie for steppin' in."

"I thought your ma was dead."

"She is. But she was gone long before she died."

Ma always steered clear of the subject of her ma, but now she was diving right in.

In public.

Comin' clean in a Laundromat.

"Why you thinkin' about all this?" I whispered. "Did something happen?"

"It's just everything." She wiped her eyes, and after another quiet spell she said, "I guess sometimes it's the parents doing the abandoning, and sometimes it's the kids."

I chewed on that a minute, but it didn't explain a thing. "What kids?"

Ma was digging through her bag. "I need to call Ellie," she said, standing up with a fistful of coins.

Which made no kind of sense to me, either.

She started to hurry off but stopped long enough to shoot me a pair of arrow-eyes. "Don't you ever leave me alone in a place with seventeen cats, you hear me, Lincoln Jones? Don't you dare."

Then she swept out the door.

A sly-eyed drifter came up to me while Ma was off phoning Aunt Ellie. "Spare some change?" he asked. He looked like he'd been shovelin' dirt for about twenty years, so using money for a wash and dry would have been putting it to good use. But I could tell from his eyes that's not where it'd be going. They were watery. And red. And when he blinked, it seemed slow and painful. Like his eyelids were lined with bits of sharp glass.

"Can *you*?" I asked back. "'Cause I got nothin'.""

I worked at making myself look bigger than eleven. Like, maybe, thirteen. And he did back off, but then he stood skulking around, checking me over with his painful eyes.

I tried to ignore him and get back to my story, but I couldn't concentrate with him there. He was scary. Not in a big-bear way. More in a sneaky-snake way. Like any minute he might pull out a knife and strike.

"Git!" I finally told him. "I got nothin'!" It just sort of popped out and made me feel like I'd bit my own tail. To my surprise, though, he took one last painful look around, then left.

I played what had happened over and over in my mind, and it kept getting better. Soon I had teeth that were flashing like diamonds when I said, "Git!" and there were actual energy beams shooting from my eyes to his. Beams that could lift him off the ground!

By the time Ma came back, I had been made Supreme Leader of Laundrovania and was using my magic energy-eyes to excavate secret tunnels behind dryer portals—escape routes that the frightened citizens of Laundrovania could use if the Drifter returned with an army of derelicts.

"Sorry that took so long," Ma said, getting busy folding clothes.

I hadn't noticed the dryer'd stopped tumbling, but Ma didn't scold me for slacking. She just set about folding like a machine, getting my T-shirts stacked while I got busy pairing up socks, wondering why she'd run off to call her sister. Her eyes looked a little puffy, but she was acting . . . solid. Like there might have been a leak, but now things were dammed up tight.

"You talk to her?" I asked.

"Mm-hmm," she said. She smoothed out a T-shirt. Snapped out another. Folded it, too, then smoothed it flat.

"So?" I finally asked.

"So . . . we're in a good place. Better'n we've been in years." She snapped out another shirt. "Maybe ever."

"So . . . she invite us for Thanksgiving?"

Ma laughed. "No, but that's a good thing." She slid a look my way. "Besides, I'm working, remember?"

I stared at her, then got back to sorting socks.

It was a whole lot simpler than sorting out Ma.

20

Magically Delicious

Early the next morning, Ma left for her half day of work like she does every Sunday. And I would have rolled over and gone back to sleep like *I* do every Sunday, only then I remembered.

There were Lucky Charms in the kitchen!

It was a mighty miracle that I'd talked Ma into buying them, but they'd been in the specials aisle with a big cutout leprechaun's talkie bubble saying, "Magically Delicious!" and a sign boasting $2.50 for the giant size.

"Please, Ma?" I begged, and after a pause that included a sigh, a frown, and one stretched eyebrow, she said, "Just this once," and put a box in the cart.

She wouldn't let me touch them when we got home, though. "A treat for Sunday," she'd said.

But now it *was* Sunday!

It was dark out, with everyone but Ma still snoozing off Saturday, but that didn't change the day. It was Sunday! And there was a giant box of magic deliciousness and a whole gallon of milk right over there! How could *anyone* sleep through that?

I ate the first bowl, feeling nothing but happy. The second bowl, I slowed down a little, giving the marshmallow stars and moons a little time to soften while I thought about my story. I'd already written six pages, but I still wasn't sure if the Ninja Cat Woman was good or evil.

It was weird not knowing. And after a while it crossed my mind that maybe she was both. Or somewhere in between. But thinking that made me feel like I was wearing a scratchy shirt that needed switchin' out of. And quick!

So I poured myself another bowl of Charms, got my notebook, and got back to the Ninja Cat Woman, hoping she would show her true colors if I kept going. But after writing two more pages, I was feeling itchier than ever, and my stomach was killing me. I'd gobbled up half the Milky Way, and now a whole constellation of moons and stars was expanding at light speed inside of me. I was dying to get up and *do* something.

Ma has only one rule for me on Sundays, and every Sunday she repeats it: "Don't you leave the apartment, Lincoln Jones." She'll usually tack on something cheerful, like, "There's folks out there who'd kill you for your empty pockets." And when I ask her, "Who'd do that?" she'll say,

"Lord, child, think! Folks who don't know your pockets are empty! And that's about everybody out there!"

One time it was, "Don't you leave this apartment, Lincoln Jones. I don't want to have to peel your splattered body off the street." So I told her, "I know how to cross a street, Ma!" and she hit me back with, "But not everybody behind a wheel knows how to drive!"

So that's how she makes sure I don't get antsy to go anywhere. And usually, staying inside is not a problem. Usually, I sleep in and laze around and then read something or write a story. Usually, I love Sunday mornings and being alone and safe in my own place with new groceries.

It's my favorite part of the week.

This Sunday, though, was different. It wasn't even ten o'clock and I was sick of everything. I didn't want to read, the Ninja Cat Woman story was going nowhere, and I sure didn't want to eat.

And then a little voice started pointing out that Ma hadn't done her usual don't-leave-the-apartment scolding on her way out the door. Maybe she'd still been caught up in thinking about her sister and just forgot. Or maybe she'd figured the rule had already sunk deep enough inside my skull. Or maybe she couldn't think of any new terrible thing that might happen to me if I left the apartment.

The little voice got a little bigger, reminding me how Ma had left me alone at the Laundromat and nothing bad had happened. Ma was probably starting to see that she didn't need to fret so much. That I was fine on my own. *Responsible.*

'Course, if I actually went off and got splatted on the street, my poor mangled body would get whupped to Sunday.

Next Sunday, which, believe me, would be a whole lot of whuppin'.

My brain was doing double shifts, though, and what it worked out was that next door was the place to go. I could offer to lend a hand to an old lady . . . who had cats! And since I wouldn't be leaving the apartment *building* . . . how could Ma be mad?

So I got up and walked out of the apartment without looking back.

Or locking the door.

Or checking to see if there were chunks of Charms stuck in my teeth.

21

The Admiral in Undies

When my knuckles hit on Mrs. Graves's door, my heart also started knocking.

And it got to knocking *hard*.

It was stupider'n spit, I know, 'cause I wasn't doing anything *wrong*. And I wasn't going to get *hurt*. Mrs. Graves was an old lady. And right next door! What could happen?

But in my brain Mrs. Graves had suddenly transformed into the Ninja Cat Woman. She had secret moves. *Stealthy* moves. Moves that could kill you.

The door didn't open with the first knock, but that didn't surprise me after the way she'd taken forever to answer it the morning before.

Maybe she was switching out of her ninja costume.

So I knocked again, louder, and my heart knocked louder, too. "Mrs. Graves!" I called. "I'm here to help!"

I stood there staring at the door, waiting for something to happen, and when nothing did, I put my ear up to the flaky paint.

Right away I heard a sound.

It was like sandpaper on wood.

Scratching.

I stooped down low and called, "Hey, kitty, kitty!" through the door, then put my ear against it again.

I heard more scratching, but now there was a voice, too. It sounded a long ways off and I could make out only one word.

Help.

"Yes, I'm here to help!" I shouted, stretching out the words like old folks need you to do. "But you have to open up."

I put my ear back on the door.

"Meowwwww, meowwwww," scratch, scratch, scratch, "Help!"

"Ma'am?" I called. It just slipped out. Like I didn't know what else to say because I didn't quite believe what I was hearing.

"Help!" she called back.

It was a jittery sound. Weak and wailing.

Like a trapped little lamb.

"Do you need help?" I called back, still not sure what to do.

I listened again, and the cats were going crazy meowing and scratching, but through all that I heard, "Help!"

The doorknob wobbled in my hand like it might fall

apart, but it didn't turn. So I rattled it and twisted harder, but it still didn't give.

"I'm coming!" I hollered, then stepped back as far as I could and charged the door, ramming it with my shoulder.

All that did was put a mighty dent in my arm and make my shirt flaky with paint. "Ow!" I yelped, my arm already throbbing.

Now I was mad at the door for hurting me, so I stepped back and kicked it, *bam*, right next to the knob, just like they do in the movies.

Swoosh, the door swung open!

Reeeeeeeeerrr, the cats went flying!

And before the cats could even think about escaping, I was inside, closing the door. "Mrs. Graves?" I called, not seeing her anywhere.

"Here!" she cried. "The door's stuck!"

It was the bathroom door, and I only had to lean into it a little before it squeaked open.

"That does it," she said, marching out in nothing but a shirt and saggy undies, acting like she was ready for battle. "That door is coming off!"

"Ma'am?" I asked, looking away from her and her saggy undies.

"I was trapped in there all night!" she snarled. "That door needs fixing, and since that's never going to happen, I'm taking it off!"

"Ma'am?" I asked again, 'cause now I was testing the door, and it seemed just fine. Maybe a little sticky, but nothing a mouse couldn't nudge open.

"Don't you tell me it's fine," she said, rattling through a drawer. "Maybe it's fine for you, but you don't live here!" She held up a screwdriver. "Ha!" she cried, then went back to searching the drawer. "Why do I need a door, hmm? There's nobody here but me!"

She turned to me, gripping a hammer in one hand and the screwdriver in the other. And with her feet planted apart like they were, she looked like an action figure. Well, an old-lady action figure. In saggy undies. But she did have light-up eyes—kaleidoscope eyes, with beams of power shooting straight at me!

Then her mouth started moving. "Lincoln," she said. "Take. Down. That. Door."

Her words hit me like a stun gun. First off, she remembered my name. How could *that* be? She had to be at least ninety! Next off, she was commanding me around like an admiral squadron leader. And last off, she was doing all of that in saggy undies like it was an everyday thing that didn't matter a hoot.

The combination had me dumbstruck.

Well, except for one word that managed to sneak out. "Ma'am?"

"Here," she said, shoving the tools at me. "Take down the door."

I'd never taken down a door before. But since there were screws going into the frame at the hinges, I figured undoing them was a good place to start.

"Stop!" the Admiral in Undies commanded when I started twisting a screw. "Just pop up the pins!"

I looked at her, back to thinking she was crazy. A door didn't have pins!

"Here," she said, then led me inside the bathroom, where she flicked a bony finger at a little groove that ran around one of the hinges. "Just tap that up and pull the pin out. Do all three and the door will come right off."

I stared at the hinge in wonder. I had opened and closed doors my whole life, just lettin' them swing back and forth for me. I'd never even considered *how* they swung, but now the hidden secrets of hinges had been revealed.

By an old lady in saggy undies.

"Go on," she said. "Put the end of the screwdriver right there and smack it upward. Once it starts, it'll go easy."

I did what she told me, and sure enough, a thing like a big brass nail came up, up, up, until it popped right out and clanked onto the floor.

"Do the other two," the Admiral commanded, "while I get dressed. I'm cold as ice!"

I did what she said, and when the third pin clanked to the ground, I jumped back, expecting the whole door to fall right off. It didn't, though. It just stayed put.

The Admiral was already back, wearing faded orange pants that looked like they were as old as she was. "That's it," she said, spying the pins on the ground. "Now pull the door straight off and set it out here against the wall."

So I gave the door a bear hug and yanked, and the hinges came apart like separating gears, half still screwed to the frame, and half still screwed to the door.

I put the door down, feeling like I'd just figured out another magic trick. "Wow."

The Admiral was frowning at the bathroom, muttering, "It could have been worse, I suppose. At least I had water and a toilet." She turned to me and showed me her yellow teeth. "And a competent new neighbor."

The Mirror Cats were nosing up to me. I didn't want to scare them off, so I let myself down to the floor real slow, 'til I was sitting cross-legged.

"That's Cleo, and that's Patrick," the Admiral said.

"What about that one?" I asked, pointing under a chair where One Eye was watching us.

"That's Jack."

"What happened to him?"

"Only he really knows." She moved into the kitchen, calling, "Don't have much in the way of boy food here, but if you want soup, I'm having some. My blood sugar's down and I'm cold to the bone."

I was still up to the gills with Lucky Charms, but I wanted to buy some more time with the cats. They were so soft. And Cleo was purring, a hum low and smooth, hypnotizing me. So I told her, "I'll have a little."

"Hmm," she said, studying me.

"Ma'am?"

"Not the answer I was expecting."

Then she turned away and got busy with a can of soup.

22

One-Eyed Jack

The Admiral ate her soup by hunchin' over it with her face practically inside the bowl. She didn't look up once as she shoveled, and that was fine by me. If she had, she'd have caught me sneaking little soupy chicken chunks to the cats.

When she'd drained the last drops into her mouth, I told her I needed to get going and asked if she wanted me to take a load of trash with me on my way out.

She wiped her cheek with the back of her hand and frowned. "I don't have much."

I couldn't help giving her counter a look. It was covered with trash. Empty cans, empty paper-towel tubes, plastic bread bags . . .

"Don't touch it," she said in a kind of growl.

"But . . ."

"They come in handy," she said. "Or could."

"If . . . ?"

"You never know." She frowned at me and stood up. "You just never know."

I stood up, too, and took the bowls over to the sink, which was crazy full of dishes. And since Ma's made me a pro at dishes, I got busy without even asking.

"Hmm," she said with a frown, but instead of stopping me, she left the kitchen.

I didn't see any dish soap around the sink, so I looked in the cabinet underneath, which was damp and musty and crammed full of junk. There were a lot of old scrub brushes and ugly toothbrushes. Plus miles of crusty cleaning stuff with labels so old you couldn't even read them. But I did find a bottle of yellow dish soap, and when I stood up, One-Eyed Jack was watching me from up on the counter.

I sneaked a peek around the kitchen wall. The Admiral was sitting in a sunny chair looking out the window, so I leaned in closer to Jack and studied his permanent wink. "How'd you lose it, huh?" I whispered.

He just sat on the counter, his tail doing a lazy little twitch from side to side.

"Keepin' it a secret?" I whispered, then got after the dishes. And soon my mind was changing Jack's story. He wasn't a war soldier—he was a pirate cat. *Argh!*

"Were you in with pirates?" I asked. "Did they smack you around?"

He seemed to give me a little smile. It was only on one side, but I swear his mouth stretched up a bit.

"Or maybe one of the ship's rats fought back?"

Then I had an even better idea!

"Did an evil seagull swoop down from the crow's nest and *peck* it out?"

The half smile was long gone, and Jack was now just doin' the lazy twitch, giving me a bored one-eyed stare.

So I dived into the dishes and got lost in picturing Jack on board a pirate ship on the pitching sea, battling rats and birds and sea monsters. I ran through five fierce eye-gouging battles, the most thrilling one involving a sea serpent with scales sharp as knives.

In all the battles, Jack lost the same eye. I just kept re-setting it and starting over until the sea serpent showed up in my mind. I could just see it, scales all green and blue and shiny, slitherin' through the waves, rearin' its head, flashing its deadly black eyes. . . .

Jack was lucky he hadn't lost his life!

When I was done with the dishes, Jack was still just sitting on the counter, watching me. Winking at me. Which made me think that maybe he *did* have telepathy. Maybe he could see everything that was going on in my head! Why else would he sit still for so long?

"We need to get you an eye patch," I told him as I hung up the raggy towel I'd used for drying. "You'd look sharp in a patch."

"Mrow!" he said, and nudged right up to me.

As much as I liked hanging out with One-Eyed Jack, I knew I'd best get home before Ma did. The Admiral was snoring in her chair, so I was planning to just sneak out, but as I was tiptoeing to the door, she sputtered to life, then saw me tiptoein' and screamed.

It was a short scream, though, choked off by something in her throat. Spit? Cat hair? Beats me, but it started her up coughing and wheezing and gasping like she was bound to die.

I fetched her a cup of water quick. And after she'd got things mostly under control, she wheezed, "You're still here."

She seemed mad about it, so I said, "Yes, ma'am. I did your dishes."

"Right, right," she said, still catching her breath. Then she nodded and warbled, "You can't go. The door needs repair."

"Ma'am?"

"You broke it."

I stared at her and finally said, "You told me to."

Her top lip lifted a quarter inch. It was the most sarcastic look I think I've ever seen. But I asked, "You want me to put it back together?" even though it was tough to keep being polite with that lip curled back like it was.

"Some toothpicks should probably do the trick."

Toothpicks?

"And a bit of glue wouldn't hurt."

Glue?

I wanted to holler, "Ma! Help!" 'cause she deals with crazy all day long. But then the Admiral creaked to her feet and said, "I do appreciate you breaking it down, Lincoln. Really, I do. But I can no longer turn a screwdriver with any force, so if you wouldn't mind helping fix it?"

I almost slapped myself silly. It was the front door she was talking about, not the bathroom door!

I followed her back to the kitchen. She said nothing about the shiny-clean sink, but she seemed very pleased when she found a smashed box of toothpicks buried in the back of a drawer. "This way," she said, like she was riding a winning streak, and led me to a little room that might've once been for a washer/dryer but was now serving as the cat yard.

My nose tried closing down as my eyes stretched wide at seeing and *smelling* the four litter boxes. I looked around, but no cats were standing by to take credit for their sand-swept sculptures.

Ma would have been going, "Oh my *Lord*," but Mrs. Graves acted like she was reaching over roses instead of turds as she fetched a bottle of glue from a cupboard. "Eureka!" she said, holding it out to me.

I took it and said, "Uh, ma'am?" 'cause she was turning to go like there was nothing wrong.

She looked at me lookin' down at the sculptures, then bent a little lower to see what I was staring at. "Oh," she said. She stooped even lower. "Oh, yes. That does need attention."

It needed a whole lot more than attention.

It needed a bulldozer!

She spread open the top of a big black garbage sack that was on the floor near a food-and-water tower. The sack already had something in the bottom, but I didn't get what it was until she said, "You mind dumping them in?" And since I was just standing like a cow-eyed rock, she nudged me with, "Just pick up the boxes one at a time and empty them in here. Then we'll fill them up fresh."

So I put down the glue, held my breath, and made like a bulldozer. And when I was done, there was a whole acre of stinky desert stuffed in the sack.

"You want me to take it down to the trash?" I asked after I'd filled the boxes with clean kitty litter, 'cause who wants a big sack of cat turds hanging around?

She shook her head. "There's still plenty of room in it."

"But, ma'am, it's already mighty heavy."

"Leave it," she commanded, then nodded at the glue and said, "Let's get that door fixed."

When I'd kicked down the door, I'd busted out some screws, and the wood where they'd been was now too spread out for the screws to bite into. But Mrs. Graves showed me that shoving toothpicks into the holes and breaking them off so they were about level and then squirting in a little glue to help things hold together would close in the holes so the screws had something to grip.

After I'd repaired the first hole, the Admiral quit barking orders while I worked and started getting nosy instead. She asked me about school and where I was from, and then she asked about Ma.

"Where is your mother today? I trust she knows you're here?"

"She's at work," I said, doing a little answer dodge as I put some muscle into flushing down a screw.

"Oh? And where's that?"

"She works at"—I caught myself from saying Crazy Town—"an old-folks' home."

The Admiral was quiet for a long time. So quiet that I found myself looking to see if she was still there. Which she was.

"What are you going to tell her?" she asked, and she didn't seem like the Admiral anymore. She seemed like a cornered mouse.

"Ma'am?" I asked.

"I'm fine," she said, finding her voice. "You tell her I manage just fine."

She left while I was cranking in the last screw, and when she came back, she had a little fold of money. "Thank you for your help, Lincoln," she said, putting it in my hand. "And I trust you won't make trouble for me."

"Trouble?" I tried to give the money back 'cause I knew Ma would not be happy about me taking it. Plus, it felt like hush money. "You don't have to—"

But the next thing I knew, I was shoved outside, standing face to face with her flaky front door, the hush money still in my hand.

23

Hush-Money Trouble

The hush money turned out to be three dollars. Three measly dollars. How much hush was she expectin' to buy with three measly dollars? It was worth a pause. Maybe an extra breath. Nobody would actually *hush* for three bucks.

I should've crammed the money under the Admiral's door, but I wasn't thinking straight. What I was thinking was Snickers.

The trouble with hush money is, it comes with voices. Whisperin' voices that started whooshin' through my head.

Go! No one will know!

Yeah! You'll be back in a flash!

You deserve a Snickers!

Think of all the work you did!

Yeah! Breakin' down doors!

Takin' down doors!

Fixin' up doors!

Yeah! And think of all those dishes!

And those nasty cat boxes!

The voices went quiet for a bit, giving me time to think, like they'd told me to. I also started thinking how, according to what had happened each and every Sunday before, I still had thirty minutes before Ma walked through the door. And that the market was right downstairs! Only two minutes away!

The voices were back.

You really think she's gonna let you keep it?

You need to spend it!

Yeah! 'Cause if you don't spend it, where you gonna hide it?

And if you do hide it, what happens if she finds it?

I had to admit, those were some mighty good points.

Time's tickin'.

What're you waiting for?

Go!

I hit the stairs running and didn't stop 'til I got to the gate. Then I double-pie-eyed the street. To the left, to the right, across it, and to the left again.

No muggers in sight.

No Ma, either!

So I slipped through the gate and hurried past Levi and his ANYTHING HELPS sign like he wasn't even there.

Inside the market it was dark. Like the belly of a big bear. One that had been roaming campsites, raiding food bins, having a snack party.

It was also quiet. Like a big-bellied *hibernating* bear. Which made me feel like I should be stealthy. Smooth. Tiptoe, even.

It's dangerous to wake a hibernating bear!

I ninja'd past the liquor wall and made a quiet beeline for the candy rack. Mr. Noe was at a computer behind the counter, looking through glasses that were straddlin' the end of his nose. He rolled an eye up and over my way, then went back to looking at his computer while I studied the candy rack.

According to the prices, I could get two large Snickers. Or a Snickers and a Kit Kat. Or a Snickers and a pack of Sour Patch! Or a Snickers and Red Vines!

I love Red Vines.

It's funny how you can set out knowing exactly what you're gonna do and end up confused. And I guess I was taking forever deciding, 'cause Mr. Noe was now aiming double-barreled eyeballs at me. "How much you got?" he asked.

I showed him my money, then glanced over my shoulder.

He looked toward the door, too. "Why are you so nervous?"

"N-nervous?"

He frowned. "You steal, I prosecute."

I tried to say, "I just showed you my money!" but my

mouth was all dry and my words just shriveled up. And the longer Mr. Noe's aim was on me, the more *I* shriveled up.

What was I doing? I'd come in for Snickers. I should get Snickers! So I plopped two king-sized on the counter, shoved my bills over, and walked away with two big candy bars and some change.

Change that was now jingling in my pocket like a little tattletale alarm.

If I'd've had more time, I'd've spent the change. Or, if it'd been found money, I wouldn't have worried. But it was hush money. What was left of it, anyway. It held a story that I wasn't allowed to tell, but it jingled and jangled like *nah-ner-nah-ner* in my pocket, giving away that I had something to hide.

I tried walking smoother, but I could still hear it, deep in my pocket, metal on metal, laughing.

How do you hush up hush money?

How do you stop it from tattling on you?

Outside the belly of the bear, sharp daylight blinded me. And I was so busy squinting and thinking about hush-money change and looking over my shoulder for Ma instead of looking where I was going that I nearly tripped over Levi.

"Oh, sorry!" I said, scampering clear of his setup.

He didn't say a word, but from his half-cocked grin and the way he was eyeballing the Snickers bars in my hand, I pieced together quick that he'd been watching me.

Watching me watch for Ma.

I stood still as a statue, calculating the situation at light speed. Then I reached in my pocket for the tattler coins and locked eyes with him as I slid them into his box, giving him a silent message: *Here's some hush money. You know what I'm sayin'?*

He gave me back a caterpillar eyebrow and a twitch of a grin, speaking without saying a thing. *You call that hush money?*

His eyes swept back down to the chocolate-colored wrappers in my hand and tossed up a twinkle when they looked at me again. I heard what he was saying without him saying a thing. *A Snickers—now* that's *hush money.*

I gave him a candy bar and skedaddled.

24

Trapped

Aside from voices, the other trouble with hush money is, it comes with a price.

A big price.

I didn't know that at the time. I just knew that Ma would be home any minute, and the only place I could think to hide a king-sized Snickers was my stomach. Maybe because it was the place I *wanted* to hide it. But I was short on time, so I sat in my corner, chewing and stuffing like a skittery squirrel.

I'd been wanting a Snickers forever. And the parts were all there—the chocolate and caramel and crunchy peanuts—but it didn't taste the same. It didn't even taste good.

It tasted like gulping down fear.

When it was gone, I felt sick. Sick, and jumpier than ever. Like I was back to hiding from Cliff.

Then I started worrying about the wrapper. First I stuffed it in my pocket. But then I started thinking . . . what if it worked its way up? What if I forgot and pulled it out? What if Ma checked my pockets while I was sleeping?

So I took it out of my jeans and buried it at the bottom of the kitchen trash.

But there wasn't much in the trash bin, and I could just see the wrapper flashing to life somehow. Unfurling like a flag, surrendering to Ma as she threw something else away!

So I dug it out quick, found some scissors, and made for the bathroom like a cat escaping a hose. Two heartbeats later, "Lincoln!" came cryin' through the door. "Lincoln, where are you?"

Lightning hit my scissors and cut up that candy wrapper. "Here, Ma! Be right out!" I hollered.

"Oh, thank the Lord," Ma cried.

I pressed the toilet lever, calling, "What's wrong?" 'cause I could tell something was and I was praying it had nothing to do with me.

"It's the Man."

"Levi?" The cyclone of water was sweepin' candy wrapper evidence round and round and down the drain as dread went washing over me. "What happened to him?" I stashed the scissors quick and found Ma rag-dollin' in a kitchen chair.

She sat up some, and her hands covered her mouth as she shook her head. "They tased him."

"*Tased* him? Who did? And why?"

"The police." She looked square at me. "He was shouting and cussing and . . . and wouldn't do what the police told him to."

"What were they telling him to do?"

"To calm down and put his hands up."

"But . . . why? What did he do?"

"I have no idea. Maybe it was being surrounded by uniforms that set him off. I tried to get him to calm down, but he didn't even seem to know who I was. And the things he was saying . . . it's like he was someone else. Some*place* else."

"Things like what, Ma?"

"I don't remember! None of it made sense! He was acting crazy! He lunged at one of the cops and they tased him." She sat panting, her eyes brimming like she was going down in choppy waters. "They tased him and hauled him off."

I wanted to say, "But he was fine! I saw him! He was twinklin' and negotiating hush-money candy! There was nothing crazy about him!"

But I didn't.

I just stood there, watching Ma drown in the things she'd seen.

"It's okay, Lincoln," she said, tossing *me* a life preserver. "We don't know what's going on in that man's mind. What voices he hears. What battles he's still fighting."

I wanted to tell her everything, but I was afraid she'd freak out. Afraid she'd be mad. Afraid everything would be . . . different. So what finally came squeakin' out of me was, "You think he'll be back?"

She was quiet plenty long enough to make me squirm. Then she sighed and said, "There's got to be someplace better for him than a dirty sidewalk. Let's hope he lands there instead."

She stretched out her arms, and when she wrapped them around me, it was like she was holding on for dear life.

I just stood there with my mouth locked down tight.

Trapped.

25

Tattletale Toilet

The next morning, Ma sprang my cage. "Lincoln!" she called from the bathroom. "Why are there bits of Snickers wrappers swimmin' around the toilet?"

I was in the middle of a dream, trapped inside the corner market by a decrepit old man who was trying to tase me for sneaking Snickers to homeless folks. His Taser was slick and could shoot from a distance, but his aim was all shaky and he was shufflin' along like a zombie in short red socks, wearing a hospital gown that was gaping wide open in back. "Don't you know it'll kill 'em?" he was shouting as I dodged him. "Send 'em straight into a diabetic coma!"

"Lincoln!" Ma hollered again. "What's a Snickers wrapper doing in the toilet?"

I was glad to shake off the zombie in red socks, but now

122

my mind was dodging around for another escape route. How could there be wrapper left in the toilet? I'd seen it go down! And I'd used the toilet since! Had some pieces stuck to the sides? Had they made their way back upstream? How could this be?

"You sure it's not somethin' else brown?" I called back.

"Lincoln Jones, I know the difference between somethin' else brown and a candy wrapper." Her head popped out of the bathroom. "And I'm guessin' no 'No' means you got some explainin' to do?"

It was early, the clock said we were running late, and she was dropping g's left and right, which all spelled trouble. "Let me see," I said, buying time.

"Mm-*hmm*." She stepped aside with hips fisted and a look that said hot water was coming to a boil and she was fixin' to dunk me.

"Maybe it's like the alligators in Florida," I said, sweating over two scraps of Snickers wrapper floating in the bowl. "You know the ones that fight their way upstream 'til they pop up someone's toilet?"

"And maybe you best quit the bobbin' and weavin' and answer me."

In class, Ms. Miller taught us about the Great Divide. It's the crest of the Rocky Mountains, where rain either rolls down west to the Pacific or east to the Atlantic. An inch one way or the other and a raindrop ends up in a completely different ocean.

During the lesson Ms. Miller was already moving on to something else when I raised my hand and asked, "What if you were a raindrop and you landed smack-dab in the middle?"

I could see her mind doing a slow step back. "Well . . . eventually you would roll one way or the other."

"But what if you balanced right there *on* the Divide? Then what?"

"Then other raindrops would join you and pull you one way or the other."

"Well . . . what if they didn't?" The rest of the class was starting to whisper, but something about being a single raindrop on the very center of the crest of the Great Divide was messing with my head.

Ms. Miller nodded and said, "Then the sun would evaporate you, and you'd condense and join a cloud, and the cloud would drop you again. Eventually you would have to go one way or the other."

So maybe what I said next to Ma was on account of knowing I couldn't stay on the Great Divide forever. Or maybe it was wanting to take down the Zombie in Red Socks, who was still staggering around in the corners of my mind. But probably it was because I couldn't take another second of feeling like *I* was the bad guy who needed lockin' up.

"Do you think Levi's dead?" I asked, cringing.

"What?"

"I think I might've killed him," I confessed, gazing into the tattletale toilet.

"Child, what are you talking about?"

"I'm not a child, Ma. I'm a murderer." I turned to face her. "I gave him a candy bar. A big one."

I could see Ma's brain shifting gears, pressing the gas, then lettin' up, trying to figure out what to say. "A candy bar can't kill a man," she finally said.

"What if he's diabetic? Ms. Miller told us that—"

"Lincoln!" She was full throttle now, like the city bus gunning it into traffic, dark exhaust puffing out all around. "What were you doing with a candy bar in the first place? And more important, why were you down on the street?"

Before I could stop it, a confession came spurting out of me. It felt like I was heaving up my guts, spraying all over Ma. And just when it seemed like I was done, more would come blurting out until finally my gut was empty. Empty, and glad to be rid of the secret.

Ma just stood there, pie-eyed, like anyone would if they'd just been hurled on. And when she was sure I was done spraying the ugly truth all over her, she gave one good, hard blink and took a mighty breath.

I hunkered down, expecting the worst, but I guess what I'd spewed was too big a mess to clean up right then, 'cause she swallowed that mighty breath, squared her shoulders, and said, "I appreciate you tellin' me the truth, Lincoln. We'll sort through this tonight. Right now we best get movin' or we'll miss our buses."

"Yes, ma'am," I said, grateful to be escaping for now.

"Eat something," she hollered over her shoulder as she scurried to get ready for work.

"Yes, ma'am!" I hollered back, 'cause all of a sudden I was starving.

26

From Bad to Worse

Seems like when a day starts off bad, it only gets worse. Could be that you're so distracted by one bad move that you wind up making others. Or maybe some days are mixed into your life to prove you can survive them. Maybe it's like leveling up.

I got to the bus stop in the nick of time and shuffled on last. Everyone else found seats quick, but I was shut out cold, with kids expanding their territory when they saw me coming down the aisle, making like there was no room on their bench in case I was thinking of squeezing in.

Nothing new there.

And then I heard my name. "Lincoln! Lincoln! Back here!"

I recognized her voice right off, and a sly-eye proved that, sure enough, it was Kandi.

My day was racing along the fast track from bad to worse. Why was she even on my bus? I checked around quick for a place to sit, pretending I hadn't heard her.

"Lincoln!" she hollered again. "Back here!"

Now everyone was staring at me, and the back of the bus started treating me like I'd been drinkin' stupid water. "Dude, what's wrong with you?" "Wake up, man!" "Helllllloooo, moron . . ."

No grapes or tuna were flingin' around yet, but I was imagining spoons getting unholstered and Troy commanding the troops.

Ready. . . .

I could feel it—spoons were being loaded.

Aim. . . .

They were cocked back and quivering!

Fire!

No food came zinging through the air, but Kandi's voice sure did. "Lincoln!"

I finally looked at her square-on. She had a hand slapped down on a seat beside her. Holding it for me. There wasn't a spoon in sight.

"Lincoln!" the bus driver hollered into her big bus mirror. "Sit down!"

"Why were you ignoring me?" Kandi hissed when I took the seat she'd saved.

"What are you doing on this bus?" I asked back.

She full-on frowned at me. "Why'd I even bother to save you a seat?"

About then is when it sank in: I was in the fling zone

and no one was hurling food *or* insults. "Where's Troy?" I asked, sly-eyeing around to be sure I wasn't about to be ambushed.

Hilly Howard was sitting across the aisle from Kandi and me, messin' with her bracelets. "I see what you mean about him not answering questions," she said over me like I wasn't even there. "It *is* annoying."

Kandi gave me the stink-eye and called, "And I'm definitely annoyed!"

So yeah. Girls are confusing. First they save you a seat, then they act mad when you're sitting in it.

Kandi crossed her arms. Her little turkey-tail nails were chipped here and there, like they were tired of looking so festive. "Aren't you going to apologize?" she asked with a huff. "Or at least thank me?"

"For what?"

"Another question," Hilly said, causing trouble. She wasn't even looking at me. She was pulling at her bracelets, moving them around and around her wrist, and it made me notice that her fingernails were painted just like Kandi's, only the turkeys looked brand-new.

"See?" Kandi cried.

"Which is another question from you," I pointed out. "You're the one who never answers questions!"

Hilly quit messing with her bracelets and squared off with me. "You could start by thanking her for saving you a seat."

I nearly broke it to her that I'd rather pick tuna out of

my hair, but she leaned across the aisle and whispered, "Or how about for getting Troy kicked off the bus?" She gave me laser-beam eyes. "Not that the world needs to know that, but you should."

My head whipped back to Kandi. "How'd you do *that*?"

She got busy chipping at a turkey tail. "I told Ms. Miller."

"But . . . *why'd* you do that?"

"Because Hilly told me how bad it was. And someone needed to do something. And I'm not afraid of Troy Pilkers."

"But . . . he's gonna think it was *me*."

It came out sounding like no one I wanted to be. I didn't sound like Lamar or Lucas or any of the heroes in my stories. I sounded like a scaredy-cat.

A coward.

Hilly leaned over the aisle again. "I'm not seein' a famous journalist in him, Kandi."

"Me?" I asked, pointing to myself like the word alone wouldn't do.

Kandi smiled at her. "You'll see."

"What are you *talking* about?" I asked, whippin' my head from side to side.

Hilly gave me a look that said I was way smaller than my britches. "Kandi was up all night predicting your future."

"What?" I was gettin' whiplash from looking back and forth.

"Hilly!" Kandi cried.

"Well, you were," Hilly grumbled. Then she frowned at me and said, "You need to thank her, stupid." She went back to her bracelets again, her little turkey tails reeling them around her wrist. "Nobody liked what Troy was doing. Even if you are a dork."

"He's *not* a dork," Kandi said.

I don't know if I was sticking up for myself or Kandi, but something made me look right at Hilly and say, "That's right. I'm not."

The bus was pulling into the drop-off zone, and Hilly stood up while it was still moving. "You are until you thank her. After that, we'll see."

They both focused double-barreled stares on me, Hilly from above, Kandi from the side.

So I broke down. "Thank you."

Kandi's nose tilted back and a little air came puffing out of it. "No problem," she said, but the look she gave me said she was lyin'.

27

Girls

At my old school, recess was indoors as much as it was outdoors. What kept us in was sometimes rain, but mostly heat or it being too humid to do much but sweat. Chasing or bouncing or dodging a ball on a swelterin' day was not my idea of fun.

Besides, I wasn't any good at sports. Ma didn't like them, and Cliff—when he came into the picture—might have been good with a bat, but he wasn't interested in swinging it at baseballs.

So sports and I never really got acquainted, and that was okay. Nobody made a fuss over it 'cause lots of other kids were spending recess indoors, too. And as long as you didn't mess with stuff or start trouble, nobody cared what you were doing in a corner by yourself, which, for me, was usually reading comics.

I love comics. The superhero kind. Which aren't funny, but for some reason they're still called comics. Ma bought them for me once in a while, but my old school's media center had a secret stash of them in a back room, and Mr. Willard, the librarian, slipped them to kids who asked. "Here you go, Mr. Jones," he'd say with a wink, and I'd be glued to the thing any chance I got.

On the back cover of every comic Mr. Willard had taped a list of vocabulary words. Words that were used in the comic. That was good for when you were reading and didn't know what a word meant, but the payback was you had to know all the words when you checked the comic back in.

"Ready, Mr. Jones?" Mr. Willard would say in a voice all hushed and secretive. Then he'd run through the list, sweepin' the room with a sly-eye as he went down it, like any minute the two of us might be hauled off to the principal's office.

"Why're there such hard words in comics?" I asked him once, 'cause after a while my brain was loaded up with vo-cab-u-lar-y.

"Because they're really for adults," he whispered. "Ready for another?"

At Thornhill there are no comics. On the second day of school I asked Ms. Raven, hoping she might have a secret stash like Mr. Willard had, but the answer was no. And when I asked Ms. Miller where indoor recess was held, she gave me a strange look and said, "We do recess outside."

I walked away feeling funny inside. Like I was alone in the middle of a school full of kids, with no place to go.

So I found a secret spot off to the side of the blacktop between a building and a fence, and that's where I'd go to work on my stories at recess. No one bothered me or even knew I holed up there.

That is, until Kandi went and messed things up.

"Why are you always hiding back here?" she asked during morning recess on the day she'd invaded the bus. She was holding on to a four-square ball and had Macy Mills and Lexi Simmons with her. They were havin' a polka-dot day. Just lookin' at them made me dizzy.

I'd jerked when Kandi had asked, 'cause I was already jumpy, worried that Troy might pop up out of nowhere and let me have it. But her asking like she did also shocked me. How long had she known about my spot?

"You want to play four square with us?" she asked.

"No thanks," I said, shaking my head.

She frowned. "If you don't watch out, you'll wind up like Isaac Monroe."

"Who?"

But they were already running off.

I grumbled, "Great. Now I'm gonna have to find a new spot." But I couldn't figure that out right then, so I got back to my story. The Ninja Cat Woman was moving through the shadows of the city's night streets, tailing a sneak thief who had stolen Old Yeller—a yellow diamond worth over a million dollars. I was putting in double agents and heart-pounding twists, so it didn't take long to forget about Kandi and four square and where Troy Pilkers might be lurking.

When recess was over and we were lined up outside the classroom, I noticed a lot of whispering behind me, but I didn't know it was *about* me until we were sitting in our seats and Colby clued me in.

"You shouldn't be writing about us," she hissed across territories. "It's not nice!"

"What?" I said, 'cause it was like a snake had struck out of nowhere.

"You heard me," she hissed.

Rayne was next to me, fiddlin' with a hair ribbon, and Wynne was across from me, wringin' the life out of a Kleenex, looking every which way but at me.

"I'm not writing about you!" I said. "Not any of you!"

"Prove it!" Colby said. She had whipped out her feather pencil and was now leaning across territories, shaking it at me like she was about to cast some deadly feather spell.

"Colby!" Ms. Miller called from the front of the class. "Put that away this instant!"

Colby put it away with a huff, but her attitude didn't go away with it. She was shootin' eye darts at me the whole rest of the morning. Then at lunch she and Rayne and Wynne surrounded me at my table. "Prove it," Colby demanded.

Rayne and Wynne still weren't looking at me, but they were there, which meant they were in the same camp as

Colby. And looking around, I saw they had backup, including Macy and Lexi and their zillion polka dots. Lots of other kids were staring at me, too. It was like a mob out there, armed with plastic pitchforks, itchin' to do me in.

I couldn't believe it. Was this what I got for minding my own business?

Was this what I got for writing in a notebook?

The whole school hated me?

It felt like I was in an oven, roasting. And since I could see only one way to bust the door open and escape, I pushed my notebook forward. "Here," I said.

Colby snatched it like she had every right to have it, and for a split second I panicked, remembering my story about Queen Colby and the spaceship. But that one had just been in my head—I hadn't actually written it down.

They huddled over my notebook like a three-headed monster, gobbling up pages while I sat there feeling mad and embarrassed.

"Who's Agent Leroy?" Rayne asked.

"What's a Ninja Cat Woman?" Wynne whispered.

They flipped through the notebook fast, until Colby finally said, "These are just . . . stories."

I yanked my notebook back. "See? Nothing in there about anybody!"

They stared at me, *sorry* written all over their faces.

And then, like someone had waved a magic wand, *poof,* Kandi appeared, rosy-cheeked and out of breath. "Guess what?" she said, sitting beside me.

Colby got right in her face. "You can't sit here! That's what!"

"Why?" Kandi said, looking all hurt.

"Leave!" Colby said, and now Rayne and Wynne were leaning in, too, like a flock of crows swooping down on roadkill.

Kandi gave me a look that was crying out for help, but I wanted nothing to do with her or the trouble she'd caused. And since I could tell I was on the verge of saying something either stupid or mean, I grabbed my stuff, gave the whole bunch of them a scorching look, and took off.

28

Catfight

It was probably stupid to think that my disappearin' into a beanbag chair for fifteen minutes meant my problems would disappear for good.

The fifteen minutes was nice, though. Agent Leroy had ducked through a maze of corridors and was now tailing the Ninja Cat Woman, who thought she was tailin' a double agent! I even laughed out loud once 'cause the picture in my head was so funny.

Then lunch was over and I went back to class in time to see Colby shove Kandi. They were over by the Golden Rule board, but I guess it's hard to read about doin' unto others when you're coming to blows, 'cause Kandi cried, "Hey!" and shoved her back, hard.

Benny Tazmin—who sits by the United We Stand wall

and had just before lunch been scolded for "disruptive behavior"—jumped up and called, "Catfight!" and seemed super excited that someone besides him might be getting in trouble.

"Girls! Girls!" Ms. Miller cried. "Stop that!" She broke them up like a referee sending boxers back to their corners. "Now, what is the problem?"

The rest of the class was moving in for a better look. "I'm sick of her spreading rumors!" Colby said, shooting eye darts at Kandi.

"I wasn't spreading rumors!" Kandi cried. "I was trying to help!"

"Help?" Ms. Miller asked. "Help who?"

A turkey-tail nail shot out in my direction. "Lincoln!"

I tried to stop my eyes from gettin' big and my face from screwin' sideways, but they just wouldn't stay put.

Benny pointed at my face and laughed, "Dude, that's priceless!" which made everyone else laugh, too.

I tried to do a face erase, but Colby kept the horror going. "He doesn't need help," she shouted at Kandi. "You just can't stand that he ignores you!"

How had this happened? All I'd done was mind my own business.

"Girls!" Ms. Miller cried. "Calm down!"

Her words had the opposite effect on Kandi, who burst into tears and went flying out of the room.

Ms. Miller sighed and said, "All right, everyone take your seat." Then she went over to the classroom phone and called the office.

The rest of the day was awkward. Kandi didn't come back, and although Ms. Miller tried acting like nothing had happened, she was the only one. Notes were slippin' around like they'd been buttered, and anytime I looked, I caught someone staring at me.

Not at Colby, at *me*.

They weren't mean looks. Not like I was trapped in enemy territory. It was more like I was some weird animal in a cage at the zoo.

When the end-of-school bell rang, I bolted out of there. I checked over my shoulder every two minutes on my way over to Brookside, making sure nobody was tailing me, and I was finally starting to breathe a little easier when Kandi stepped out from behind a tree and planted herself in front of me.

"Aaaah!" I cried, jumping back. "Noooooo!"

"Do you hate me?" she sniffed.

"Yes" and "Leave me alone" would have ended things right then, but she was still crying, and her eyes were all puffy, and most of her turkey tails were completely chipped off. Which added up to me saying, "No!" like I actually meant it.

Sometimes I really am dumber'n dirt.

"Stop walking," she whimpered. "*Please* stop walking."

She sat down on a concrete step near the tree and patted the space next to her. "I'm really sorry. I was just trying to help!"

I wasn't about to sit down, but I also couldn't stop from asking, "Help with *what*? Troy? It doesn't help that now he has an actual *reason* to be mad at me! And tellin' folks I was writin' about them . . . I told you that wasn't so!"

"I told them you were a journalist," she whimpered. "I was trying to make it sound important! I didn't know the difference."

"What difference?"

"Between a journalist and someone who makes up stories!" She grabbed a stick off the ground and started jabbing at the dirt. "Colby told me."

"But why'd you tell anyone *anything*?"

She shrugged. "I was trying to help."

"Help with *what*?"

"Friends."

"Friends?"

"Lincoln," she said, looking at me like I was a poor, dying puppy, "you have no friends."

My cheeks got hot and my eyes pied out, and for the second time that day I could not do a face erase.

And then with a sniff, she gave me a look that was all parts sad. Like she felt just awful about breaking the news to me. "The people in your stories are not real, Lincoln."

I could feel my whole face go hot. "What do you know?" I shouted, then started running away from her as fast as I could.

29

Walker Wars

I used to have friends. That was back before Cliff. After Cliff I was too busy hiding what he was like from my friends to notice I was losing them. I didn't want them knowing the trouble I'd been in. I didn't want them seeing the marks on me, which sometimes took weeks to clear up.

So I hid the cryin' and started lyin'.

Back then, I believed the things Cliff yelled at me—that him being mad was all my fault. I thought *I* was the reason he was hurtin' Ma.

Back then, I didn't understand about whiskey time.

By the time Ma figured out what Cliff was up to while she was at work, I was used to doing the hush-and-hide. And her trying to fix things only made it worse for me when she wasn't looking.

One of the places I'd go to hide was inside my stories. I could be there for hours, quiet as a mouse. And when I was in the middle of an exciting part, or when the jail cell was about to clang loud with the sound of justice, I didn't miss having friends. The friends I made up were enough.

So Kandi saying what she did felt like a sucker punch. What did she know? About any of it?

I was madder'n a hairy hornet, but once I was at Brookside, I got distracted by what was going on in the East Wing.

Two oldies named Linda and June were facing off, fighting over a walker. Linda was on the inside of the walker, scooting forward, shouting "Move!" at June, who was on the outside, grabbing the crossbar, shouting, "Give it back! It's mine!"

Linda wasn't about to. She shoved forward. "Move, you old coot!"

Two oldies fighting over a walker wasn't anything new or shocking. What was new *and* shocking was these two doing it. Linda and June were best friends and usually quiet, zoning out in front of the TV holding hands. But now they were shooting killer eye darts at each other, actin' like they'd wrestle to the death over a walker.

I looked around for a Purple Shirt—any Purple Shirt— but Ma and Gloria weren't in the Clubhouse, and neither was Teena or Carmen.

Then Debbie Rucker shouted, "What is your name?" at

me, and Suzie York came up asking, "Do you know how to get out of here?" and Crazy Paula started tapping on the table like she was sending out a frantic message. And through all that, the Walker War was escalating.

"It's mine!" June shouted, shaking the bar.

"Let go, or I'll flatten you!" Linda yelled, shoving forward.

"Catfight!" Teddy C called, sounding mighty gleeful from the comfort of an easy chair.

Across the room, Debbie Rucker turned up the volume. "WHAT IS YOUR NAME?"

So I shouted back, "LINCOLN!" And since no Purple Shirts were showing up, I put myself in the middle of the Walker War, telling the battling oldies, "Now, now," just like Gloria would have.

"Tell her to let go!" Linda shouted.

"Tell her to give it back!" June shouted louder, shaking the crossbar.

Across the battlefield, Debbie hollered, "Lincoln was my favorite president!" while Suzie York tugged on my sleeve and begged, "Get me out of here!" and Teddy C cheered, "Catfight!"—this time from up on his feet.

In the nick of time, Gloria came running out of Mrs. White's room and saved the day. "June Bug, dear! There, there! What's wrong?"

"This thief stole my walker!" June snarled, keeping her eyes locked on Linda. "And now she's saying it's hers!"

Gloria put her arm around June, and in a real soothing

voice, she said, "Have you seen your zucchini? I think one might be ready to harvest."

"Is it?" June asked, turning to face her.

"Mm-hmm," Gloria said, gently pulling one of her hands off the walker. "Lincoln can show you."

I gave Gloria a look like, I can? But she gave me a pleading one back and whispered, "Mrs. White's roommate just passed. . . . It would help me so much if you could—"

"Sure," I said, calculating that Ma was probably inside the Psychic Vampire's room and, with another roommate down, there wasn't enough garlic on the planet to risk leaving her alone in there.

So the next thing I knew, the Walker War was over and I was headed outdoors with Looney June to find a zucchini. *Shuff, shuff, shuff,* we walked, with her holding on to my arm and me thinking that walking old folks was not something that should be left to the young. It hurts to walk that slow. You can feel yourself growing old, walking that slow.

Right outside the patio door, there's a sunny table where the same small group of oldies hangs out on any nice day. There's Sir Robert, who Ma says is not really a sir or named Robert. There's Alice, who calls everyone sweet pea and claims she feels naked without her pearl necklace. And there's Pam, who has little pom-poms strapped to her walker and wears a cheerleader top of some kind or another every single solid day. The school it's from doesn't matter—if there's a megaphone on it, it'll do.

Alice may dress all proper, but she's trouble. She's worse than Teddy C, 'cause instead of a whoop or a whistle, Alice grabs your backside.

I'm not fooling.

The first time she grabbed mine, I whipped around, not believing what had happened, and she said, "Hello, sweet pea," and gave me a wicked grin.

The next time, I told her, "Don't do that!" and she just laughed and said, "Do what, sweet pea?" which made her and Pam laugh like a couple of wrinkly-faced hyenas.

Now I just swing wide when I have to walk by her. And that's exactly what I was doing when Sir Robert called out, "Good evening, m'lady!" to Looney June.

"She's no lady!" Alice snapped at him.

"Certainly not," Pom-Pom Pam said, sizing June up with a frown.

But June had her eyes on Sir Robert, who was all decked out in his usual button-down shirt, with a silky scarf tucked in around the collar. "Good evening!" she said with a little bow.

"Where are you off to on such a glorious evening?" Sir Robert asked.

June's smile wilted as she tried to remember. Then it boinged back to life and she said, "Why, right here!" and headed for the only empty chair at the table.

"No!" Pam said. "You can't sit here!"

Alice grabbed the arm of the empty chair and pulled it away from June. "Go away!"

And I was in the middle of thinking that Brookside was just like school but with wrinkles when a voice behind me said, "Lincoln?"

I could feel my blood do an instant curdle, and when I turned around, sure enough, it was Kandi.

30

Jailbreak

I stared at Kandi like I was seeing ghosts, my mind holding its cheeks, screeching in terror at the sight of her. How could this be? What was I gonna do? There was no escaping the way this was going to haunt me at school.

"How'd you get in?" I choked out.

"I told them I was your friend," she said, looking around. "And I met your mom. She was, um, disposing of diapers?"

"You are not my friend!" I said through my teeth. "You're a stalker!"

"Lincoln," she said, like a pouty little puppy. "I'm just trying to *help*."

"Go away!"

But now Sir Robert and the ladies were all tuned in.

"Hello, sweet pea," Alice said, twiddlin' her pearls as she checked Kandi over.

"Beautiful hair," Pom-Pom Pam said.

Alice nodded. "I could rule the world with hair like that."

"I once did!" Pam said. "I could grow it for miles. Best hair on the cheer team, hands down."

Alice let go of her pearls and scowled at June. "Good thing your granddaughter didn't inherit *your* lousy hair."

June looked confused. Like she wasn't really sure who these people were or why they were being mean to her.

Kandi was keepin' quiet, which was a relief until I saw that she was soaking it all up like a giant sponge.

The same way she'd soaked up my story.

That put me skidding into a double worry. How could I stop her from spreadin' this all over school?

"Guess you won't be needing this," Alice said, yanking the chair free from June.

"Yes, have a nice walk," Pam added.

They were telling us to move along clear as a ringin' bell, and with the chair yanked back, June was now hanging on to me for dear life.

"Where are we going?" June asked as I pulled her along.

"To look at your zucchinis, remember?"

"Oh, that's right," she said.

We shuffled down the walkway a few steps, and I guess latching on to one arm wasn't enough for her, 'cause she grabbed Kandi's, too, turning us into a human walker. "I'm glad you're here," she said, smiling at Kandi. "Do you want to see my zucchinis?"

"Sure," Kandi said, smiling back.

Then June asked her, "How's your mother?"

"My *mother*?" Kandi looked like she'd been goosed, then turned to me with question marks flashing.

I faked like I didn't see.

June frowned. "Why doesn't she ever visit me?"

"Visit you?" Kandi asked, sneaking pie-eyes my way.

I gave her a dark look, which was all she deserved after nosing her way into Crazy Town.

"It'd be nice to get a visit from her every now and then," June said with a huff. "Is that too much to ask?"

Kandi, for once, was speechless.

"Well," June said, shuff-shuff-shuffing along. "It's nice that *you're* here, dear, even if your mother can't be bothered."

"Who *is* this?" Kandi mouthed at me.

Which earned her another dark look.

The "courtyard" at Brookside is a maze of walkways that go winding around the Activities Room and the two wings. It's where the oldies get their sunshine and go for walks. There are nice plants and garden decorations, but if you look past the flowers and trees and fake squirrels, you start to see that you're trapped inside the walls of a fort.

As we shuffled to a T in the walkway, where the choice was to go left toward the garden and the West Wing or right to a dead end, we saw about six oldies congregating at the dead-end fence.

I didn't recognize any in the group, and for a minute I thought the guy in the middle might work at Brookside. He had a head of thick brown hair and didn't look *that* old, but then I saw he was wearing pajama pants. And he was barefoot.

The rest of the group were all women, and even though they were trying to whisper, they were fighting about something.

"No! I get to go first!"

"No, *I* do!"

"He said *I* could!"

Pajama Man was trying to look over the dead-end fence but couldn't reach high enough. So he gave up and said, "Line up!" in a gruff voice.

Two of the women had walkers and they jockeyed to get up front, but a tall lady in pink pants elbowed her way in.

Pajama Man was stooped over now with his hands laced together.

"What are they doing?" Kandi whispered.

"Escaping," I whispered back, forgetting that I was givin' her the silent treatment.

Pajama Man tried to give Pink Pants a boost, but she couldn't seem to push herself up. And then there was a rush of feet from the left and a man's voice shouting, "Stop!"

"Quick!" the oldies all cried. "They're coming!"

"Sergeant Baker!" the man who was running shouted. "Sergeant Baker, stand down!"

Pajama Man straightened up, then drooped, his whole body a flag of surrender.

The others grumbled, and a couple of them cussed, but

they all turned away from the dead end and started shuffling back toward the West Wing like a litter of naughty puppies.

Gloria hurried up behind us, and when she saw that the group was heading back to the West Wing, she let out a big breath and asked me, "Maybe you can take June inside?" Then she smiled at Kandi and said hi, and eyed us back and forth like she was trying to figure out the situation.

"I'm Lincoln's friend," Kandi said, lying through her teeth. "It's nice that he comes here every day, isn't it?"

"It sure is," Gloria said, giving me one of her sweet smiles.

Then Kandi asked, "Is everyone here . . . ?" and she wiggled a finger around by her head.

"Oh, yes," Gloria said with a laugh.

And that was it.

I was doomed.

31

A Day Full of Learnin'

As soon as Kandi got what she wanted, she was gone. I was left feeling like a skunked dog, knowing that kids at school were gonna start holding their noses around me and whispering behind my back. *Did you hear? Lincoln spends his afters in a looney bin! His mom works there changing crazy geezers' diapers!*

Ma wanted to know who my friend was, and she asked like it was something exciting.

I went at her like a snapping turtle. "She's *not* my friend! I hate her!"

Ma tried finding out more, but I shut her down. And since she was still on the clock, she left me alone at my table, where I pictured everything that would happen at school the next day over and over in my mind until it felt like *I* belonged in Crazy Town.

With all that had happened at school and after, I'd forgotten about what had happened before—about the Snickers and Levi and the tattletale wrapper.

Ma hadn't.

My first reminder was when I saw Ma pack up leftovers. That made everything else flood back and made me want to stay put at my table in Crazy Town, even though Paula was tapping, and Debbie was shouting, and Ruby was trying to pull off her clothes.

Anything was better than facing Ma about the Snickers.

But instead of lighting into me like I'd been dreading, Ma was quiet on the walk to the bus stop. And then *on* the bus, she was still not acting mad when she said, "There's something I need to explain to you."

I waited, not sure where this was going.

"You're eleven," she said.

It didn't sound like she was asking this time, but she did have a worried look on her face. Like my being eleven might be a deadly condition. "So?"

"So if something happens to you while I've left you home alone, they could take you from me."

"What? Why?"

"Because here you need to be twelve to be left alone."

"Why?"

"It's the law. Ellie told me. I didn't believe her at first, but I checked, and it's true. And if social workers found out you were on your own and saw where we're living . . ."

"What's wrong with where we're livin'?"

Her look threw me back into the zoo. Only instead of

making me feel like some freak creature in a cage, this look said I was something cute and cuddly. "Ma! Why you lookin' at me like that?"

She kissed me on the forehead and sighed. "Oh, Lincoln."

This was definitely not going the way I'd expected. And something about that made me blurt out, "Ma, I'm sorry for sneaking out, okay? It was just downstairs. That's all."

"I'm more worried about the lying."

"I didn't lie!"

"You did some pretty fancy dodging, which has the same intention."

I looked down.

"I'm also worried about where you got the money."

I frowned and thought hard about how to answer.

"Lincoln. Tell me."

"You have to promise not to . . . not to *do* anything."

"Do anything like what?"

"Like anything!"

"Child, if you're gettin' mixed up in—"

"I'm *not*. I'm not mixed up in *anything*. I got three dollars for helping an old lady, okay?"

The rest came busting out like a sack of marbles scattering across the floor. I told her about breaking down a door, taking off a door, and fixing up a door. And I tried to hold back about the kitty litter and garbage and the three dollars being hush money, but that all clattered out, too. By the time I quit talking, my sack of secrets was empty.

I held my breath, watching Ma collect all the things I'd said. She seemed to be picking them up one at a time.

Carefully.

Putting them inside a sack of her own.

"Ma," I said. "Mrs. Graves doesn't want folks knowin'. Or interferin'."

Ma nodded. "Like I don't want folks knowin'. Or interferin'."

What she was saying took a second to sink in. "You mean with us?"

"Mm-hmm." She shook her head. "But with us, you're getting bigger and stronger. With her . . . it's just downhill. And if she can't even open her bathroom door . . . ?"

"That's not a problem anymore." I frowned. "She doesn't want to wind up at Brookside."

Ma frowned back. "She'd be lucky to wind up at Brookside. Most places aren't near as nice as Brookside."

"So why's Suzie York always lookin' for a way out?"

Ma kept quiet.

"Besides, Mrs. Graves remembered my name. And it's not like she can't throw out her garbage. She just doesn't want to."

"And why's that?"

"She . . . she's waitin' for the stuff to come in handy."

Ma leveled a look at me, then shook her head again and sighed. "Lincoln, she needs help."

"*She* doesn't think so!" I leaned back and crossed my arms. "And after today, I'm done with folks meddlin' in my business, and I sure don't want to meddle in theirs." I shot her an arrow-eye. "Or have a ma who does."

She checked me over. "Does this have to do with that girl?"

I gave a snort, and on the subject of Kandi Kain, that's all I was spillin'.

When we got to the corner market, Levi was not in his spot.

Another guy was.

The new guy was younger but had long stringy hair and watery eyes. His sign said:

WHY LIE? I NEED A BEER!

Ma offered him the wrapped-up leftovers, and he took them but didn't thank her. And after we'd set off toward the gate, the food came flying at us, hitting Ma in the back. "I ain't no *dog*," he yelled.

Ma grabbed me when I made like I was gonna clock him, and she pulled me along quick, without even looking back.

After we'd ducked through the gate, she held still a minute, then took a deep breath and said, "It's been a day full of learnin'."

It seemed crazy to me that she'd say that after being smacked in the back with leftovers.

Then again, it seemed like the only sane way to sum up the day.

(32)

The *Bulletin*

It wasn't until we were eating supper that I thought to ask. "The Psychic Vampire struck again, huh?"

Ma's head wiggled. "It's unbelievable." She lowered her voice like she was afraid Mrs. White might hear. "You know what she said to me?"

"What?"

"'No one's taking *my* window seat!'"

"She said that?" My voice was whisperin' now, too. It all seemed so creepy.

"Mm-hmm." She leaned in a little. "She claims folks come in at night and beat her up so they can get her spot."

"Beat her up?"

"But she fights them off."

"She can't even sit up!"

Ma sat back. "Well, she's holding on to her window, I can tell you that."

I gave that a minute, then asked, "So who's next?"

"There's talk of leaving the bed empty."

"Really?"

"Mm-hmm." She scooped up some stew. "Despite the waiting list."

"Seems to me there's a big waitin' list to get *out* of that place," I said. "You should have seen the crazies trying to climb the fence today!"

She frowned. "I heard. Gloria spotted them on the monitor."

"The monitor?"

"The whole outside's covered by cameras. You never noticed?"

I shook my head. "So there's no hope of them escapin'?"

"Hope? What do you mean, hope?"

"They're never gonna bust free?"

She was quiet, picking around her stew for a minute. "They're not prisoners, Lincoln."

I about sprayed my food. "Tell that to Suzie York. Or to that Sergeant Baker guy."

"Who?"

"The guy giving crazies boosts over the fence!"

She frowned. And when she spoke again, it was quiet, but in a way that was tellin' me to hear her loud and clear. "You need to stop calling them crazies. They have dementia."

"That's just a nice way of saying they're crazy."

She went on like I hadn't said a word. "And if they did get out, they'd be lost or dead in no time. They're like children, Lincoln. Someone needs to care for them."

Questions went flyin' through my head. Like, *Well, who put 'em in there? Why don't* they *take care of them?*

But those questions also sent *pictures* flying through my head. Pictures of crazies, living with us. Paula at our supper table, tapping. Debbie off in a corner, hollerin', "WHAT IS YOUR NAME?" Any one of them leaving puddles on the furniture or screamin' bloody murder in the shower or flingin' food around the place—all stuff I'd seen at Brookside.

Instead of asking my questions, I said nothing. But Ma was quiet, too, which usually means a talk is brewing.

Sure enough, right before bed Ma came and sat on my mattress. She had some folded papers in her hands and said, "The folks living at Brookside weren't always crazy."

I just nodded, wondering which way this was going.

"I know it's hard to picture, but they were once eleven, just like you. And I promise you, they never thought they'd be living at Brookside."

A vision of kids from school all shriveled up and hunched over walkers popped into my head. Colby's walker was decorated with feathers, and she looked like an old bird, hobbling along. Troy Pilkers was yellin' stuff and hurling food, Hilly Howard was in a corner, staring at her bracelets, and Kandi was bossing everyone around, teeth clacking and diaper showing.

"I've been reading these," Ma said, pulling me out of my

nightmare. "They've helped give me understanding and patience when I'm about out."

"What are they?" I asked.

She handed them over. "Every one of these has a 'Resident Spotlight.' That's the part to read."

"What's a Resident Spotlight?"

"You'll see. Just read." Then she stood up and went to bed.

When I unfolded the stack, I found myself face to face with the *Brookside Bulletin*. On top was the November issue, behind it was October, behind that, September and clear back to June—back to before Ma was even working there.

The front page of the November issue had a boxed-in part about Veterans Day, inviting folks to come to a celebration honoring the veterans who were living at Brookside. The date was already past, and I sure hadn't heard anything about it, but according to the newsletter, the celebration included refreshments and a movie called *Flags of Our Fathers*.

It sounded like a party.

Outside the box there were three announcements about November activities, with headlines reading FOL-LIES TO PERFORM AT BROOKSIDE and EXPERIENCE THE JUNIOR JAZZ TRIO and LORI'S CASUALS FASHION SHOW.

I stared at the page, wondering if this was the same Brookside I'd been going to every day.

Then I turned the page and saw big bold letters announcing RESIDENT SPOTLIGHT—the part Ma had told me to read—and saw that the article was about Paula.

Crazy, tapping Paula.

There was a picture of her looking just like I knew her. But none of that matched a whole page of small print about her. It was written by her two daughters and started with where Paula was born and about her family, where she grew up and went to school—regular stuff. But then it told how she'd worked for thirty years as a civil rights attorney and loved to go rock-climbing.

By the end of the article, my jaw was dangling. I could not picture Crazy Paula rock-climbing. Or working as a lawyer! All I could see was a shriveled-up woman with drooping eyes, tapping.

So . . . maybe all that tapping came from hearing the judge slam a gavel for thirty years. Maybe that sound was stuck so deep in her brain that it was the last thing to go.

But . . . an *attorney*?

What had happened to her? Had she fallen off a rock and hit her head?

I went back to the article and found out that, no, she hadn't hit her head. She'd just slowly lost her mind.

When I was done with that Resident Spotlight I read the others, and they were all just as flabbergasting. I learned that Peggy Riggs used to teach calculus, Mrs. White had done missions in Africa, Droolin' Stu used to be a mechanical engineer, and Suzie York had six kids and seventeen grandkids.

"Ma?" I called, and when she didn't answer, I went to her room. "Ma?"

"What is it?" She was in bed, sounding mighty drowsy.

"Why do some old folks lose their minds and others don't?"

She propped up a little. "They don't really know. But they're trying to figure it out."

"Who is?"

"Scientists. Doctors. Folks like that."

"So it's not from drinking too much booze or hitting your head or eating aluminum?"

"Eating aluminum?"

"Well, drinking soda out of a can. Someone told me once it can give you Alzheimer's."

She laughed a little. "Well, I don't know about that. And liquor and hitting your head won't *help*, that's for sure, but Debbie Rucker's the only one at Brookside I know of who had something like that happen. A blood vessel broke in her brain."

"But . . . why'd that make her want to know folks' names?"

Ma yawned. "The brain is complicated, Lincoln. I'm not sure anyone can really answer that question." Her eyes were drooping, but she patted the bed, and when I sat on it, she held my hand and said, "I only want two things from you regardin' this, okay?"

I nodded, waiting.

"Appreciate being young. I know that can be hard, but you'll be old soon enough, and there's no goin' back."

I nodded. "And?"

"And quit callin' them crazies. They can't help the state they're in."

I looked down.

"Is that a 'Yes, ma'am'?" she asked, and one eyebrow was cocked way up.

I nodded.

"So let's hear it."

"Yes, ma'am."

She gave me a pat. "Now go to bed."

Something I was more'n happy to do.

33

Facing the Truth

I woke up knowing I had to survive only one day of Troy Pilkers tracking me down and Kandi Kain spreading stories about me at school before having five days off for Thanksgiving break.

Just one day of duckin' and dodgin' and five days of *ahhhh*.

Then Ma went and monkey-wrenched me.

"You're going to have to come with me tomorrow and Thursday. And Friday," she said, bustling around the kitchen.

"What?"

She tased me with a look. "Got wax in your ears, child?"

"Ma! You can't be serious!"

"Where else you gonna go?"

"I'll just stay here!"

"No, you won't."

"But, Ma!"

"Get movin'. I can't have you missin' the bus."

The bus was about to leave when I got to my stop, but the driver saw me coming and flapped the doors back open. And when I ran up the steps, she gave me a wink and a grin. "Good morning, Lincoln," she said. "We should be smooth sailing for the rest of the year."

"Ma'am?"

She leaned over a little and lowered her voice. "Our problem is definitely not returning." She gave me another wink and wagged her head to the back of the bus. "Go on."

I moved along but my mind was a jumble. Had the bus driver known all year that food was flingin' in the back of her bus? And if she had, why hadn't she kicked Troy off the bus a long time ago?

Or maybe she knew something was going on but couldn't peg what. Maybe she found food splats all over at the end of the day and cursed whoever was doing it. Maybe Kandi tattling was the break she'd been waiting for all year.

As I walked along looking for a seat, I got a sick feeling in my stomach. Not like the one I got every day, knowing I was moving toward the fling zone. This one was from feeling like a coward. I hadn't stuck up for myself—I'd just taken it. Instead of swattin' at the bee, I'd let it sting me, over and over and over. Things hadn't gotten any better with me ignoring Troy—they'd gotten worse.

Until Kandi had come along and stuck her nose in things.

I was smashed between the gears of wanting to throttle Kandi and knowing I should thank her for real. Like I meant it.

It was a terrible place to be caught.

Hilly was waving from the back of the bus. "Hey!" she called. "Back here!"

I moved along, acting like a snake might jump out and bite me, but I did end up sitting next to her.

"So?" she said, twiddlin' her bracelets.

"So?" I said back.

"How are things with you and Kandi?"

I slid her a look. "Painful."

"Ooooh," she said, reading way too much into one word. Then she slid me a look back and said, "Well, you should be nicer to her."

Her telling me that sent me in the opposite direction. "I'm plenty nice to her!"

She crossed her arms and full-on looked at me. And after she got done sizing me up with a frown, she said, "If that's your idea of nice, then no wonder you don't have any friends."

"What? How would you know about my friends? How would you know anything?"

She just shrugged and went back to messin' with her

bracelets, and I turned away from her, feeling hot and mighty angry.

And then Ma's voice started running through my head.

On our long bus ride escaping Cliff, Ma told me that in fights, nothing makes a person madder than the truth. "Anger won't change the truth. It just works like a drug that makes you feel better for a while. But no matter how much you yell or blame or how many fists you throw, the truth'll be there waiting for you when you sober up. The only way out is to face the truth and try and fix things."

It had started off with her talking about Cliff but had turned into something that felt bigger than him. Her eyes were drilling into me as she spoke, and her voice was powerful in how quiet it was. Even as tired as I was, I could tell she wasn't just explaining things.

She was *warning* me.

I didn't really understand why on that bus, but as I got off this one, it hit home.

I was mad.

I was plenty mad!

But the sick feeling in my stomach was coming from the truth.

A truth that had nothin' to do with anyone but me.

34

Steamed

It was a complicated feeling. One that I sure wasn't going to be able to sort out before class started. On the one hand, Kandi had gotten Troy Pilkers kicked off the bus. On the other, she had spied on me, followed me, and nosed her way into stuff that was none of her business. And worst of all, she *talked*. What a mess she'd made, tellin' folks about my writing. And now that she knew where I went after school, everybody would know!

I headed for the media center to hide out, picturing how the day would go. I could just see it—kids whispering, their eyes scooting around, watching me. That grew into me imagining kids whispering and pointing, with nobody even bothering to do the sly-eye. Soon my mind was in a house of terrors, with kids ballooning in size, pointing and laughing. *HHHA-HA-HA! HHHA-HA-HA!*

Then a voice broke into my house of terrors. "She's kidding, right?"

Poof. The laughing kids disappeared, and I was outside the media center with a real boy standing right next to me. The one I'd seen working at Ms. Raven's computer.

His hair was wild, and his backpack looked like it weighed more than he did. He was grabbing the shoulder straps tight. "It's going to be closed all day?" he said, pointing to a sign taped to the door.

I would have been upset, too, but I got distracted by the strap where his hand had been.

It had a name written on it.

Isaac Monroe.

A bell went clanging inside my head. And then Kandi's voice started clanging beside it. *If you don't watch out, you'll wind up like Isaac Monroe.*

I stared at him, trying to figure out what Kandi had meant. He looked pretty normal to me. Well, except for the backpack making him look like a pack mule. And his hair making him look like a wild sea anemone.

"Why are you staring at me?" he said.

"I . . ." But before I could think of something to say, he clomped away.

I could feel my cheeks burn. I hadn't just been looking, I'd been fool-faced *staring.* And even though I was kicking myself for doing it, I was mostly mad at Kandi.

Why'd she have to say anything about Isaac Monroe?

Why'd she go around talking about folks?

Thinking that made *all* of me hot. Like steam was

building up inside of me. The feeling I'd had on the bus was long gone. This was *Kandi's* fault. If she had just left me alone with my stories, nobody would've thought I was writing about them! But she nosed and nosed and then went and said stuff like, *If you don't watch out, you'll wind up like Isaac Monroe.* Even before I knew who he was, I thought there was something off about Isaac Monroe, all because of Kandi.

Well, Isaac Monroe might look like a wild anemone pack mule, but at least he didn't paint his fingernails like candy corn or turkey tails!

I steamed along looking for Kandi 'cause I'd had enough. And I knew what she was doing! Right that instant she was tellin' someone that Lincoln Jones's ma worked in Crazy Town.

Like it was anyone's business?

It wasn't hard to find her. She was on the playground talking to a group of kids—boys and girls—waving her hands through the air and laughing.

The other kids were laughing, too.

I ran at them, full speed ahead. "Stop it!" I shouted, plowing into the group like a runaway train. I looked right at Kandi. "Stop nosing in other folks' lives, stop following them around, and stop talking about stuff that has nothing to do with you!"

Kandi did stop.

Everybody else stopped, too.

And they all stared at me.

"You think it's something to make fun of," I shouted, "but it's not!"

Kandi blinked at me, not saying a word. But the other kids started asking, "What's he talking about?" "Make fun of what?" "Why's he so mad?" "Kandi, what's going on?"

Kandi just shook her head, then turned and gave me those stupid puppy-dog eyes. Like, *Oh, you poor, sad boy.*

"Stop that!" I shouted at her. And because it felt like the world wasn't quite spinning the way it's supposed to and I needed to get my footing back, I said, "And what's so weird about Isaac Monroe?"

Everybody turned back to Kandi.

"I never said he was weird," she said softly. "He's just . . . a loner."

"So what?" I shouted.

"Calm down, Lincoln," she said. "Really, it's okay." Then she leaned in and whispered, "I didn't tell anyone anything."

When it sank in that she was telling the truth, an *oops* flattened out my face. And when I stepped back, I saw that the group was about twice as big as it had been when I'd come crashing in. Colby was there. So was Benny. And Hank and Troy. And Rayne.

"What's wrong?" Rayne asked.

"Nothing," I said, backpedaling, then running away.

What I meant, though, was *everything.*

35

Half Sweat, Half Shower

I was mighty relieved when school let out. Not that anything happened during it, but I kept expecting it to, which was maybe worse than if it actually had.

I kept my radar up for Kandi on the walk to Brookside, but she didn't pop up anywhere, and neither did Troy. I almost jumped for joy when I made it to Brookside without being ambushed.

The minute I was inside, though, I came skiddin' to a stop. Thanksgiving decorations were all over the place. There were full-on hay bales and cornstalks, but it wasn't like being on a farm. It was all *fancy*. Like a scarecrow dressed in a tux and wearin' shades.

Geri said, "Nice transformation, isn't it?" And after I'd signed in, she hurried around from behind her desk. She was wearing little white sneakers and blue jeans and moving faster than usual. "Wait until you see the Activities Room! It's almost ready for tomorrow."

"Tomorrow?" I asked.

"For our Thanksgiving celebration?"

"But . . . tomorrow's Wednesday."

"That's right. We do it on Wednesday so families can celebrate here with their loved one and have their own celebration on Thursday." She keyed in the pass code. "It works out better that way."

"Wow!" I said, taking in the Activities Room, which had been made into a dining hall, with white tablecloths and Thanksgiving decorations everywhere. "Who did all this?"

"The activity director's in charge, but everybody helped out. It's fun and festive, don't you think?"

I nodded. "It looks great."

"You're joining us tomorrow, right?" She gave me a sweet smile. "You're family now, too, you know."

"Uh, yes, ma'am." And I should have left it right there, but the "family" part was messin' with my head a little, so I let slip, "Ma says I have to."

Geri laughed.

"I didn't mean it like that!"

She chuckled. "Believe me, I understand." Then she keyed me into the back door of the East Wing and said, "But we'll have a great time, I promise."

The back hallway of the East Wing looked the same as usual—not a stick of Thanksgiving decoration. I could hear snifflin' comin' from down Dove Lane, but that wasn't anything shocking. Tears spring up quick at Brookside, but if Gloria's nearby, a few *there, theres* and they disappear just as fast.

But when I glanced down Dove Lane, it wasn't one of the oldies doing the snifflin'. It was Gloria. And Ma was the one standing by, making soothing sounds.

"What's goin' on?" I asked, and right away Gloria flicked back her tears and said, "Oh, nothing, dear."

Ma was a little more truthful. She scowled down the hallway and said, "Wilhelmina's son says we're doing a slipshod job of taking care of his mother."

I knew who Wilhelmina was. She stayed in her room most days, but according to Ma, she was a terror. She hit and bit and screamed bloody murder over everything. Ma would come out soaked after bathing her. "Half sweat, half shower," she told me on a bus ride home. "Lord save me from having to bathe that woman ever again!"

I spy-eyed the hallway toward Wilhelmina's door. "Doesn't her son know how much trouble she is?"

Gloria put on a brave smile. "She's been here a year, but this is his first visit. He can't know what we go through."

"But he should," Ma growled. "And him threatening to have us fired? That's . . ." Ma's head wobbled and steamed and looked mighty close to exploding.

"Can he do that?" I asked.

Gloria shook her head. "It just hurts to hear. Especially when you try so hard."

Ma finally spouted off. "Who does he think he is any-way, comin' in and bossin' us around like that?"

"Uh . . . Wilhelmina's son?" Gloria said with a shaky little grin. Then she took a mighty breath and grabbed Ma by the arm. "Come on. We should get back to it."

It didn't take long for Gloria to make like she was over what had happened, but I could tell something was still knotting her up. She kept checking the main East Wing door like she was expecting something bad to come bustin' through it. And then she came up to me all fidgety and asked, "Dear, would you mind playing with them?" She was pointing out a table where Pom-Pom Pam and June were sitting with an oldie named Marla, putting together Scrabble letters on the bare table. "They lose their way. And I can't handle a squabble right now. Not with"—she gave the door a worried look—"all I need to do before tomorrow."

"Sure," I told her, and went right over, filling the fourth seat at the table.

"Oh, good," June said to me, then pointed at a word that would have put me in hot water if I'd've said it at home. "Make her take it off."

"If it's in the dictionary, it's fair play!" Marla said, giving me a twinkle. "And that baby's in the dictionary!"

"It's crude," June said, reaching for the word. "And I'm taking it off!"

Marla slapped her away. "Hands off!"

"Now, now," I said, putting them back in their corners, like I pictured Gloria doing. "It's Pam's turn, right?"

They all gave me the wary-eye, but finally nodded.

At Brookside, players don't bother to hide their Scrabble letters. They keep them faceup in front of them, but it doesn't seem to affect the play. I guess it's hard enough for them to make words without worrying about anything else. So since I could see Pam's spread of letters, I pointed to her *L* and said, "You don't have to take off Marla's word, just change it with that."

"Ha!" June chortled. "Do it! Do it!"

So Pam turned the word to "LASS" like she was making a royal move, and then Marla went and shocked everyone by saying, "Now *that's* how you play. Good move."

I was feeling mighty proud for snuffing the fuse of that situation when a man walked into the Clubhouse. He was wearing slacks, polished shoes, and a tucked-in polo shirt, and he was talking on his phone.

I'd never seen him before, but I knew right off that he was Wilhelmina's son. I could just tell. He was keeping his voice down, but it filled the room with a low growl, and he was moving like a dog fixin' to bite.

Which I guess is why nobody stopped him when he started going inside bedrooms. Most of the doors were wide open, but even the ones that weren't he opened anyway, doing a quick tour before moving on to the next one.

Ma and Gloria stayed back, twitching as they watched him. Teena and Carmen were steerin' clear, too, delivering laundry to rooms he wasn't anywhere near.

After seeing him go in and out of so many rooms, I

started getting a dangerous case of the snoops. What was he doing?

When he went into Mrs. White's room and didn't come out, I could see Ma and Gloria whispering, wondering if they should go find out what he was up to.

Or maybe they were hoping Mrs. White was using her vampire powers!

A few minutes later he was *still* in there, so I got gutsy and went over and spied through the door. My heart was jumping like a jackrabbit, but his back was turned, so I held still and listened while he talked on the phone.

"They better not have a problem with it," he was saying. "Why would they? The second space is empty! . . . No, it's not by the window, but the woman in here is on hospice and doesn't look like she'll make it through tomorrow. . . . Why wait? We pay a lot of money to have her here! . . . Well, I think it *is* reasonable to demand that they move Mom now. She doesn't like her room, and her roommate *moans*. Have you heard it? It would drive me crazy! And this one's just lying here like she's already dead! . . . Well, I don't care. This is a much better room, and when this roommate goes, we'll make sure Mom gets the window. . . . Well, isn't that typical of you? . . . No, *you* listen. You're not roadblocking me on this! I don't care if you are the legal authority, I'm not leaving here until I get her moved!"

He jabbed at his phone, and I ducked to the side quick, but he never even noticed me. He stormed out of Mrs.

White's room and snapped his fingers at Ma, commandin' her to let him out of the Clubhouse.

When he was gone, Ma and Gloria both swooped down on me. "What did you hear?" they whispered.

So I told them, and they listened with their eyes stretched high and their mouths stretched low.

When I was done, Ma whispered, "He said all that? Right there by Mrs. White?"

"Yes, ma'am."

"Lord!"

Gloria looked toward the main door. "I'll bet he's gone to talk to Mr. Freize. And I'm sure he'll get his way." But when she turned back, I could see she was trying to fight off a tickling at the corners of her mouth.

Ma noticed it, too. "Gloria?"

Gloria shook her head a little, but the tickle wasn't letting up. And finally she said, "Poor Wilhelmina."

Slowly, Ma's mouth took up the tickle.

Mine did, too.

Poor Wilhelmina.

36

Good Shirt Math

Ma got off work really late. Partly that was because of moving Wilhelmina into Room 102—something her bossy son watched over the whole time. And partly that was because of everything that needed doing before the next day—giving oldies showers, mostly. And tidying up. And readying clothes for any oldie whose family was coming to the Brookside Thanksgiving.

"Why's everything got to be so perfect?" I asked on the bus ride home.

"Some folks only visit on holidays. It's important the residents look their best."

"But . . . isn't that like faking it?"

"It's the same as cleaning yourself up before family comes to supper." She looked out the window. "Just a whole lot more work when a body has trouble moving on its own."

I was going to leave it right there, but she turned back and stared at me.

"What?" I asked.

Behind her stare, I could see tired wheels turning toward trouble. And before long she took up blinkin'—something I knew to be a dangerous sign.

"No, Ma. Whatever you're thinkin', no. There's only so much one day can take."

But she yanked on the stop cord, and before I knew it, we were off the bus miles from home, marching along the sidewalk.

"Where we goin', Ma?"

"To fetch you some clothes. I'm wearin' my work uniform tomorrow, but you can't be showin' up in that."

I was tripping all over myself to keep up. "I've got clean stuff at home!"

"Did you see Brookside today?" She tossed me a look that was half angry, half helpless. "I had no idea all this would be such a fuss or I'd have planned better." She started walking even faster. "Lord, I hope they're still open."

"Who, Ma?"

But then we turned the corner and I knew.

Goodwill.

The lights were on, and we made it with seven minutes to spare. And in seven minutes, Ma tracked down some slacks, a button-down shirt, and a pair of shoes. The shoes were at least two sizes too big, but it was the only pair that came anywhere near fitting me. "Better too big than too small," Ma said, and headed for the register.

The clothes came to six dollars and fifty-two cents. That left Ma with a little change from the seven dollars she handed over, and left me with an eye on the stack of comic books by the register. They were tattered and torn, but I heard them crying out, *Lincoln . . .*

"They're only a quarter, Ma, please?" I begged.

Ma looked at me, at the change in her hand, at the comics, and back at me.

I could feel my face start to crumble.

That was not her cavin' look.

That was her stand-firm look.

But . . . why? She had a quarter right there in her hand! And couldn't she hear the comics calling my name?

And then the girl behind the counter said, "One free comic book with the purchase of a traditional Thanksgiving outfit."

I stared at her, not believing my ears. She had eyes that looked like they'd lost a battle with a fat-tipped Sharpie and had pins sticking through an eyebrow, but her voice was like angels singing.

"Go on," she said. "Take one."

She didn't have to say it again.

Back on the bus Ma leaned against the window and closed her eyes. "Four of those comics equals one good shirt," she said, sounding worn to the bone.

I knew she was explaining why she hadn't jumped at

the chance to buy me a comic, but it gave me an instant case of guilt over the hush money I'd wasted.

I tried to smooth it all over by kiddin' around. "So . . . can I take the shirt back?"

Her head turned toward me. Slowly. Like it was in need of oilin'.

"You're a funny boy, Lincoln Jones."

"Yes, ma'am," I said, grinning at her.

She raised a disapprovin' eyebrow, then turned back to the window, but I could see her in the glass, smiling.

The next morning we were up early, same as every Wednesday, but instead of getting on the school bus, I got on the city bus with Ma. My Goodwill clothes and comic book were in my backpack, along with a notebook for stories.

"So," Ma said once we were settled in, "I've been thinking."

"Not already . . . !" I moaned.

"What am I gonna say?" she asked, her proper tone instantly slippin' away.

"Somethin' havin' to do with me doin' somethin' besides readin' my comic book?"

"Hmm," she said, sizing me up. "How'd you know?"

"Ma!"

"And didn't you read the whole thing last night?"

"It was a speed-read! To see how it ended! I need to go back and read it right."

She sighed. "Look, Lincoln, I didn't ask if it was okay for you to spend the whole day with me. I figured it'd be fine, but after all the fuss yesterday, I don't want to jeopardize my job."

"But Gloria said—"

"Gloria's been workin' there five years and everybody loves her. No one's firin' Gloria." She took a deep breath. "Me, I'm new, and not as . . . sunny as Gloria."

"So . . . why was she the one so shook up yesterday and not you?"

Ma gave me a long, hard stare, then nodded and said, "I guess we can thank Cliff for that."

"What's Cliff got to do with this?"

"I'm done takin' the blame for stuff I haven't done. I'm done with Cliff and anyone like him, which means I ain't cowerin' to the likes of Wilhelmina's son."

My jaw went for a tumble. "You think he's as bad as Cliff?"

She gave a little snort. "Same animal, different claws. I don't know what he said to the director, but he got Wilhelmina moved like *that,* so I think he's got a way of gettin' what he wants. And last night he wanted me and Gloria fired."

"But—"

"I cannot lose this job, Lincoln. So I'm gonna stand my ground, but I'm also gonna make sure I don't give Mr. Freize some other excuse to fire me." She turned double-barrels on me. "So if you don't mind, I've been thinkin'."

I swallowed hard. "Yes, ma'am."

"I need you to be helpful today. Helpful and cheerful. No broodin' about bein' at Brookside on your day off, no callin' folks crazies. I want you to help with the snacks, help clear the dishes, do table activities with the residents, or just sit and talk with them. Make like you're happy to be there, and be *thankful*." Her lips pinched together hard, and I could see tears springin' up in her eyes. And finally what she was thinking came slippin' out around the rock choking off her throat. "Remember last year, and be thankful."

Funny how you can move away from a place, but the memories of it move right along with you. Suddenly my mind was at last year's Thanksgiving, with me hiding from Cliff under the table as he went after Ma, yelling at the top of his lungs, "Orange glaze don't belong on a Thanksgiving bird! You know I hate sweet with my meat! How am I suppose'ta eat that?" He had her up against the wall, spraying whiskey breath in her face. "Answer me, woman! How?"

I would have tried to make him let go of her, but the times I'd done that before, he'd sent me flying across the room and then doubled down on Ma. So I held my breath and waited while Ma choked out, "Sorry," over and over until Cliff finally shoved her aside.

"I'm glad you got us out of there, Ma," I said.

She gave me a little smile, but I could see she was still battling the rock in her throat. So when she started turning back to the window, I touched her arm and said, "I am thankful, Ma. Mighty thankful. And I'm happy to help."

She raised an eyebrow. "Remember that when Paula starts tappin'."

I raised one back. "And Debbie asks what my name is?"

"And Peggy starts talkin' to the air."

"And Alice grabs my backside?"

Both Ma's eyebrows went flyin'. "She does that?"

I laughed, "Don't worry. I've learned to steer clear."

She laughed, too, and something about seeing her head thrown back with laughter made me feel lucky.

Lucky to be spending the day with her.

Even if it was in Crazy Town.

37

The Demon Gasp

Ma's shift started with the news that Wilhelmina was definitely still alive.

So was Mrs. White.

"Oh, Lord," Ma said when she heard squalling coming from Room 102.

"Can you get that?" Gloria called. She was dealing with Teddy C, who was spittin' out his dentures and cussin' up a storm.

"Sure," Ma called back, and for some reason I followed her inside the Vampire's suite.

"She's not getting my window!" Mrs. White wheezed. She was looking straight up like she was talking to the ceiling. "Tell her! She can't have my window!"

Wilhelmina was standing by the window. The hair on

the back of her head was mashed flat like someone had lifted a boulder off a field of dry grass. "What is she doing in my room?" Wilhelmina demanded, turning to glare at Mrs. White.

"*Your* room?" Mrs. White hacked out. "This is *my* room!"

Wilhelmina gave Ma a look that oozed like a cut onion. She pointed at Mrs. White and said, "Get. Her. Out!"

"*You* get out," Mrs. White wheezed. Her head creaked toward Ma. "Arrest her!"

"Arrest *me*?" Wilhelmina cried. "They should arrest you for making me feel like I'm in a death ward!" She glared at Ma. "Why is she here?"

I could see Ma box away all the mean things Wilhelmina had said and done to her. I could see her reminding herself that Wilhelmina was ornery because she was confused and frustrated. Frustrated over losing her mind.

Ma grabbed a framed photo from Mrs. White's side table and shoved it at me. "Distract Mrs. White while I take Wilhelmina out of here."

I almost blurted, "No! Not me!" but a fierce look from Ma set me moving to Mrs. White's bedside with the photo.

The Vampire was even scarier close up. Her teeth were brown and her hands were bony bird claws. I could see blue veins crossing her almost-bald skull like a road map, and there were little patches of raw skin spotting her face.

She was back to looking straight up and hadn't seen me yet, and I had an urge as big as Texas to run. But I'd promised to help, so I looked at the picture in my hand, tryin' to figure out what to say.

Most of the oldies have pictures of their family surrounding them. I've seen Gloria and the others pick up a picture and hold it in front of an oldie and say, "Is this your daughter?" or "Tell me about him," or "My what a beautiful bride you were!" and get them talking about something happy.

In her whole half of the room, Mrs. White had one picture, and I was holding it. It was a group shot of a bunch of boys on a patch of bone-dry dirt in front of a hut. The boys had on no shoes and barely any clothes, but they were laughing and smiling. In the middle of the boys was a woman dressed in safari clothes, and her smile was even bigger than the boys' smiles.

And I was just wondering if the Safari Lady might be Mrs. White's daughter when I flashed back to what I'd read in the *Brookside Bulletin* about Mrs. White being a missionary in Africa.

I looked at the Safari Lady closer. And closer. She looked nothing like the Psychic Vampire. But . . . why else would this picture be here?

"Is this *you*?" I asked, showing her the picture.

I must have startled her because she jerked a little. Then her claws reached out for the picture, and for the first time, her eyes turned on me. They were blue and so faded. Like a sky burnt to white by summer heat.

And then suddenly the sky started rainin'.

"You're here," she said, her eyes spillin' over. "I thought you'd never come."

She rested the picture in her lap and reached a shaky hand over, grabbing mine.

It was like a corpse coming to life, and my mind was screamin', *Zombies! Run!* but the Icy Bird Claw of Death was *clamped* on. "Please stay," she begged.

My mind was reeling in terror. Was this how she pulled the life force out of folks? Was I the Psychic Vampire's next victim? But much as I wanted to run, there was something about her watery eyes that kept me in place.

"How are the others?" she asked, looking back at the picture and then at me. "Are they here, too?"

I've seen Ma and Gloria do the smile-and-play-along with the oldies enough to know it's the best way to keep things from breakin' down. So I tried, "The others are fine. But no, it's just me."

The Weepy Vampire held on tighter. "Sit with me."

I looked over my shoulder for help, but Ma was long gone, and since the Vampire's grip was deadly and her eyes were on me like laser beams, I sat in the chair by the bed.

"Thank you," she said through her cracking lips.

Her head creaked back to center, so at least she was looking straight up again instead of at me. But even though her eyes had released me and were closing, her hand was still clamped on tight.

Holding the hand of an almost-corpse is plenty creepy, but when the hand may be pulling out your life force, it's also *scary*. And piled on top of creepy and scary was painful, since my hand was stretched and twisted over the bedrail.

I sat there watching her breathe, waiting for the chance to slip free. I could see the ribs in her chest go up and down, up and down, like they were trying to poke through her tissue-paper skin.

I read once that birds have tendons in their feet that keep them clamped on to a wire or perch when they sleep. They don't have to think about it or make it happen—it's a reflex. Even though Mrs. White was still clamped on tight to my hand, she seemed to be asleep, so I pulled my hand free.

"No!" she cried, sputtering to life.

Her head creaked my way, and she looked so relieved to see I was still there that when she reached through the bars for my hand, I gave in and let her hold it. "Don't go," she croaked out. "Please stay."

When Gloria breezed in a few minutes later and saw me holding the Psychic Vampire's hand, her eyebrows went flying. "My," she whispered, like I was some sort of superhero.

It left me feeling like I couldn't ask her to help me escape, even though that's exactly what I wanted to do.

Gloria checked Mrs. White over, then tucked an extra blanket around her and told her, "Sweet dreams."

Mrs. White held on to me tighter.

After Gloria left, I rested my head against the bed rail

and waited for Mrs. White to really go to sleep. I don't know how long I sat there with her hand clamped on mine, 'cause I got lost in thinking about flying through the city like superheroes do. First I had a cape, then I had a bodysuit with an *L* for Lincoln on my chest, but folks on the street were crying, "Loserman!" so my mind erased the *L* and went for a symbol of wings instead.

Once I had the picture of wings on my chest, I sprouted them on my back. I didn't need a cape to fly—I had wings!

The wings changed everything. I became powerful and mobile. I was Angelman, and villains didn't have a chance! I swooped around the city, ridding it of evil.

But even being a superhero angel doesn't erase the creepiness of holding hands with a psychic vampire, so after a while I veeeery sloooowly pulled my hand away.

This time, she didn't budge. So I veeeery sloooowly pushed myself out of the chair. And I was veeeery sloooowly turning to go when Mrs. White's eyes flew open and a screeching sound came out of her mouth.

Or *into* her mouth.

Her jaw dropped open, her bony chest went up, and her eyes stayed cranked wide while the horrible sound happened.

It was like a demon was being sucked inside her.

"Help!" I cried, and bolted for the Clubhouse. "She's possessed!"

The oldies at the tables didn't budge or even look over, but Ma sure did. She came racing toward me, and since I couldn't *explain* what I'd just seen, I made like Mrs. White, cranking my eyes open and making a sound like a demon was entering my body.

She seemed to understand that evil forces were at work in the Vampire's room. "Stay here," she commanded, holding a stern finger in front of my face.

"You can't go in there!" I cried when I realized she was going in for battle.

"Stay!" she said, doing the finger thing again.

Then Gloria appeared, asking, "What happened?"

So I cranked my eyes and did the demon gasp again, and Gloria went in to back up Ma.

Angelman must still have been operating inside me, because I couldn't just stand by and let them battle the demon alone. I took a deep breath, puffed out my chest, and went inside.

Ma and Gloria were both standing over Mrs. White, and Gloria had just clicked off a walkie-talkie.

Good! They were calling for more backup!

Only . . . Mrs. White wasn't looking possessed. Her eyes were closed and she was back to looking like skin over bones.

Bones that weren't moving.

At all.

I said, "She was . . . she was . . ."

Gloria gave me a soothing smile. Like *I* was crazy!

"No!" I cried. "Her eyes were all cranked back and she was gasping like, ghaaaaaaagh, and—"

"There, there," Gloria cooed. "That was just her agonal gasp."

"Her what?"

Ma put her arm around me. "Her last breath, Lincoln." A nurse walked in as Ma walked me out, and that's when I finally got the picture.

The Psychic Vampire was dead.

She wouldn't be sucking up any more life forces. Or saying mean things to Ma. Or screeching at folks about her window.

She was dead.

Finally dead.

And the confusing thing was, I couldn't stop crying.

38

Phantom Flavor

A chill was swirlin' through me like an ice storm. I couldn't get the sight of Mrs. White or the sound of her demon gasp out of my mind, and her icy bird-claw seemed to still be clinging to my hand.

Ma parked me in the phone room and apologized all over the place for asking me to help. I told her it wasn't her fault that Mrs. White held on for nine hundred years and decided to let go while she was holdin' on to me. I tried acting like I was all recovered, but I was pretty wigged out and Ma knew it.

"Just stay in here," she said, twitching with nerves. "Just stay in here and read your comic book."

I warmed right up to that idea. And since we could hear clankin' and bangin' and Teddy C hollerin' about needin' his teeth, I told Ma, "Go on! I'm fine."

After she left, I holed up with my comic book, and it did help. A lot. But out of the corner of my eye I could see Ma and Gloria working away, and after a while guilt started pangin' through me. They were doin' a nonstop hustle in and out of rooms, changin' diapers, wiping up spills, delivering snacks, and fetching Teddy C's teeth, which he kept hurlin' across the room.

They also performed a magic trick when the medical folks were taking Mrs. White away. All they really did was talk to any oldie the stretcher needed to roll by, but it was like a hocus-pocus of smiles and words and gentle touches. I swear the oldies had no idea one of their own was dead and going, going, gone.

After that, Ma and the others started setting up for lunch, and that's when the guilt pangs took over. Ma hadn't sat down once the whole time, and here I was, lazin' around reading comics?

So I went out and helped with lunch and then was busy the whole rest of the afternoon. I did some cleaning up, but mostly what Ma and Gloria wanted was for me to hang out with the oldies, starting with Ruby Hobbs. "If you could just sit and visit with her? She's about to go tearful on us."

Tearful I could take, as long as she didn't go naked!

When I sat by her and said, "Hi, Ruby," her weepy face dried right up and she started babbling about things that made no sense whatsoever. I tried to follow what she was saying, but she seemed to be stringing random words together and I didn't have the decoder.

It must've made sense to her, though, 'cause she was smiling like she was telling a happy tale, and all I had to do was nod and say, "Wow," or "Really?" to keep her going. When she was all tuckered out from talking, she closed her eyes right there in her chair and nodded off.

After Ruby, I asked Ma what else I could do, and she said, "Just make the rounds," which meant going from one table to the next, playing cards or helping with a puzzle or just visiting. It was easy 'cause things seemed pretty much under control. At the moment, Tapping Paula was Napping Paula, Sir Robert was outside with Sweet-Pea Alice and Pom-Pom Pam, June and Linda were by the TV holding hands, and except for Teddy C—who was still fussin' about his teeth—everyone else seemed to be doing okay.

All that changed when Teena cleared away Debbie Rucker's snack dish.

"Bring it back!" Debbie shouted. "I said, bring it back! There's a lot of flavor left in that bowl!"

She was talking about a plastic pudding bowl that looked pretty scraped out to me.

Teena said, "You're done, Debbie," and kept clearing dishes while Debbie got madder and madder.

"Did you hear me? Give it back!"

"You're done, Debbie."

"GIVE IT BACK!"

Teena ignored her, piled up the dishes, and left. But even though the dish was long gone, Debbie kept shouting, "GIVE IT BACK! GIVE IT BACK RIGHT NOW!"

Ma finally came out of one of the rooms with her blue sani-gloves on. "Is there any way you can get her to quit squalling?" she begged me.

So I went over to Debbie and said, "Hi."

She was all red in the face, but she did change subjects. "What is your name?"

"Lincoln."

"What is your last name?"

"Jones."

"Lincoln Jones," she said, taking a deep, choppy breath. "Can you please bring me a pudding? They took mine away before I was done."

"They're all gone. But we're having Thanksgiving dinner really soon."

"We *are*?"

"Yes, ma'am. I heard there's turkey and mashed potatoes and stuffing. . . . It's going to be a feast."

"Really?" Her red edges were fading fast. "What about pie?"

"I'm guessin' pumpkin? Maybe apple?"

She let out a happy sigh, and her eyes got glassy. "Lincoln Jones?"

"Yes, ma'am?"

"Will you go for a walk with me?"

My eyes went shiftin' around, but my mouth went, "Sure."

She smiled and latched on to me as we headed for fresh air. "Lincoln Jones?"

"Yes, ma'am?"

"I like pumpkin pie."

"Yes, ma'am. Me too."

We walked a little further. "Lincoln Jones?"

"Yes, ma'am?"

"I love Thanksgiving."

"Me too."

Outside now, she looked up at the sky and took a deep breath. "Lincoln Jones?"

"Yes, ma'am?"

She smiled at me. She seemed so calm now. Like a different person. "I'm glad you're here."

I smiled back, and it was truly a wonder to feel the same.

(39)

Ruby's Family

Since families had to sign up to come to the Brookside Thanksgiving, the staff knew how many places to set. The tables in the Activities Room were put up banquet-style, which really meant picnic-style, with folding tables hiding under white tablecloths. Only about half the oldies had folks coming. I guess there's no sense signing up for a feast if your oldie's stuck in bed or would rather sleep than eat.

When families from both wings started arriving, Ma had me change into my new clothes, which she'd starched to practically standin' during one of her breaks. I was not looking forward to being boxed in by buttons and starch, but when Gloria saw me, I changed my mind.

"My, how handsome you look, dear!"

I could feel my cheeks get hot. "Thank you, ma'am."

The caregivers had to wear their work shirts so folks would know who to ask if they needed help, and since Ma's shift was extended to overlap with the night crew, there were Purple Shirts all over the place. Some were taking care of the oldies who were not coming to Thanksgiving, and the rest were working the feast.

"Where should I sit, Ma?" I whispered when I found her in the Activities Room. The place was buzzin' with folks, and it felt like my first day at Thornhill, where everybody but me seemed to know somebody.

Ma looked around, sizing up the place. It was fillin' in fast, and I could tell she hadn't thought about where I'd be sitting until just now.

Then, coming up behind us from the East Wing, we heard singin'.

Loud, warbly singin'.

"The hills are alive with the sound of muuuusic . . ."

We turned around, and sure enough, it was Ruby Hobbs.

"Mother," a lady beside her was saying, "we'll sing after dinner, okay?"

"With songs they have sung for a thousand yeeeeears . . ."

"Mother, shh. We'll sing after dinner."

There was a man with them, and trailing behind the three grown-ups were a sour-faced girl and a boy.

A boy I knew from school.

My forehead went poppin' with sweat, but before I

could dive for cover, Isaac Monroe recognized me. His eyes went shifty—like he wanted to duck for cover, too.

Somehow Isaac's ma picked up on the situation. "Do you two know each other?" she asked.

I was waiting for Isaac to say something, and I guess he was waiting on me, 'cause we were both standin' there, dumbstruck, when Ruby went and shocked everybody. Not by strippin', but by smiling right at me and saying, "This is Lincoln."

The whole Monroe family was staring at me now, and I could see new questions springin' up in their minds. So I dodged the new ones by answering the old one. "We go to the same school."

I could see Mrs. Monroe's mind clicking with connections. "This is your son, Maribelle?" she asked, smiling at Ma.

"He sure is," Ma said, putting a hand on my shoulder.

"It is such a pleasure to meet you," Mrs. Monroe said, sizing me up from head to oversized shoes. "I see your mother every Tuesday and Friday morning when I visit." She turned to Ma and smiled. "We're like old friends by now, aren't we, Maribelle?"

Ma gave her a smile back, but there was a twitchiness to it. Like her *face* had been starched to standing but could crumble any minute.

Mrs. Monroe had already turned to herd her kids forward. "This is Isaac," she said, directin' the introduction at Ma. "And this is Liza."

"A pleasure to meet you both," Ma said, soundin' mighty proper. Then she saw that Ruby had started to droop, and she waved the family along, saying, "You should probably go find seats. We're glad you all could make it!"

Mrs. Monroe had only gone a few steps when she turned back and said, "Are you here with other family?"

She was lookin' straight at me, so I shook my head.

"Why don't you come sit with us?" She smiled at Ma. "If that's okay with your mother?"

"That'd be very nice," Ma said, not even botherin' to wonder what I thought of it. Not that I *knew* what I thought of it, but havin' supper with a bunch of strangers was not my idea of a good time. Even if one of them went to my school.

"Come join us, Lincoln," Mrs. Monroe said, and Ma pushed me along, whisperin', "Mind your manners!"

Once we got settled at a table, Isaac's ma was friendly, but Isaac was just quiet, and Liza was in a dark mood. Then their folks started talking to the folks taking chairs next to them, and the rest of us were left sittin' around all awkward while Ruby spaced out.

"I can sit someplace else," I finally said.

"No!" Isaac said, like his voice was tryin' to stop something from falling.

"How does she know you?" Liza asked, sliding a look my way.

"Ruby?" It came blurting out before I had the good sense to stop it.

Liza looked at me like I'd stung her. "You call her by her first name?"

I started scooting back from the table. "I think I should probably go sit someplace else."

"Sorry. Not your fault," she said, stopping my chair. "Being here's just painful. First I hated Saturdays. Now Thanksgiving, too."

Isaac leaned across the table, whispering, "It's not Thanksgiving, and she can't help it."

"Like I don't know that?" Liza said, her words like spit on a skillet. She leaned forward at him now, saying, "How's your research coming? Still think you're going to find a cure?"

"Shut up!"

"You shut up!"

"Kids!" their ma hissed across her ma. "Not now! Spend a little time talking to your grandmother."

"Why? She doesn't even know who I am!" Liza hissed back, right across Ruby. Then, louder, she said, "Do you, Grandma?"

Mrs. Monroe turned up the volume, too. "Of course you remember Liza and Isaac, right, Mother?"

Ruby gave Mrs. Monroe a quivery smile. "What was that?"

"Your grandchildren! You remember Liza and Isaac, don't you?"

"I have grandchildren?"

Liza pushed back from the table. "I'm going for a walk."

"What? No!" her ma cried.

"They're not even close to serving," Liza said, and took off toward the East Wing.

Mrs. Monroe gave Isaac a pleading look, so he said, "I'll find her," like it was something he was used to being asked to do. He pushed back and looked at me, saying, "Come on."

Come on? I barely knew him. And I sure didn't want to chase down a girl who was shooting off attitude.

Best to stay away!

But . . . if I didn't follow Isaac, I'd be stuck sittin' by myself next to Ruby Hobbs, which was bad enough right there, but who knew what she'd do?

I hopped up quick and hurried after Isaac.

40

Cool Air

We found Liza outside in the dark, mopin' at the table where Sweet-Pea Alice and Pom-Pom Pam usually hung out with Sir Robert.

"Go away," Liza growled at us, her breath puffing white in the cold air. But before either of us could say a word, she leaned forward at me and said, "How can she possibly know you and not me?"

"I don't know," I said, tiptoeing through a minefield of words. "Maybe because Debbie makes me say my name every afternoon?"

"Debbie?" Her head started quivering. "Who's Debbie?"

"The one who's always shoutin', 'WHAT IS YOUR NAME?'"

Her eyes were squinting now. "Every afternoon? Are

you saying you're here *every afternoon*? Why haven't I seen you before?" She turned to her brother. "Have you seen him here before?"

Isaac shook his head.

I looked down and toed a crack in the concrete. "I'm not here weekends," I said, going with what she'd said earlier about hating Saturdays. "Just during the week." I peeked up and they were both staring at me now. "I come after school."

"*Why?*" Liza said, squinting harder.

Isaac stepped in. "Look, it's not his fault Grandma knows him. If she sees him every day, he's become part of her new memory map. Which makes sense since—"

"Stop!" Liza cried. "I don't care about any 'memory map'!"

"But it probably explains why she knows him and not us! She sees him over and over—he's part of her new memory map!"

Liza rolled her eyes. "Genius here's looking for a cure. You know that, right?" she said in my direction.

"Knock it off, Liza," Isaac growled.

"Is that what you research in the media center?" I asked.

He nodded, but he and Liza were still glarin' at each other.

So I tried smoothin' things over. "Well, someone's got to find a cure, right? Why not him?"

Isaac gave me a look that was all parts grateful, but Liza

frowned at me like I had beans for brains. "Well, let's see. For starters . . . he's eleven years old!"

"So?" Isaac said.

"So?! It's a disease, Isaac! It shuts your body down! It *kills* you!"

"I know that! Stop treating me like I'm a stupid kid. I know a lot more about this than you do! And at least I'm trying to do something about it instead of saying she'd be better off dead, like you do!"

"Well, she would be," Liza grumbled. "And she's going to be! I heard the director tell Mom that most people last here about two years. Grandma's been here a year and a half. She'll be dead before you're out of elementary school!"

Isaac's face freeze-framed, and his eyes kinda glazed over. Not like he was gonna bust out in tears, more like he was doin' some complex calculations in his mind. Finally he blinked and said, "Maybe if we took some of her DNA and—"

"STOP IT!" Liza yelled. "There's nothing *you* can do about it! And I'm sorry, but I don't want to hear any more of your crazy ideas or your technical explanations for why she knows *him* and not me!"

"Not *us*," Isaac said with a frown.

"I know, but I'm older. I've known her longer. She saw me every day after school since I was in kindergarten! And before that she saw me the whole day while Mom and Dad were at work! I should be mapped into her brain so deep she could never forget me!" She turned a glassy look on me. "But no. She knows *him* and not me!"

"She doesn't *know* me," I said. "She's never said my name before. I was as shocked as you. And I bet if I went in there now, she'd look at me like she'd never seen me before."

Liza stared at me for a solid minute, then sighed and leaned back in her chair. "How do you take being here every day?"

"It is pretty crazy," I said.

Liza snorted. "Talk about an understatement."

"But none of 'em's my kin, y'know?"

"Your *kin*?"

I looked away, not wanting to get grilled about what hole I'd crawled out of. "Family. None of 'em's family."

A cloud of quiet moved in and hung overhead until Isaac asked, "So your mother's a caregiver?"

I shrugged. "Every day but Saturdays."

"I can't believe you come here every day," Liza said. "Do your friends know?"

The question felt like a bee sting, and she must've seen how uncomfortable it made me, 'cause she snorted and said, "Yeah, people judge. Even when you try to explain, they just don't get it."

I thought about the truth in that. How if someone had told me even a little of what I'd seen while spending my afters at Brookside, I'd have laughed or hurled or called them a liar.

But seeing it day after day?

Watching what the Purple Shirts go through?

Having Mrs. White die holdin' my hand?

I got it, all right.

And I was pretty sure I wouldn't be forgetting it any-time soon.

41

Zombie in a Wheelchair

Isaac checked his watch and said, "We should get back," but it was probably more the cold than the time that got Liza up and moving. Her teeth were actually chattering when she said, "Good idea."

Problem was, we were locked out. The door we'd come through had been propped open before but was now closed up tight, and knocking brought nobody to our rescue. Even after pounding, nobody came.

Liza took up worrying between banging on the door. "What if they started serving? Mom's going to be so mad! Why isn't anyone in there?"

Through the door window, I could see Droolin' Stu sittin' in his corner and Peggy Riggs on a couch talking to air, but other than that, the place looked deserted.

I was itching to punch in the code and let us inside,

but I stopped short of doing it. I reminded myself that the only good secret is a kept secret, and this sure didn't seem like anything worth jeopardizing Ma's job over.

So after Liza banged again, I said, "Let's try another door."

"Fine," she huffed, and started running away from the East Wing and around the corner toward the back side of the Activities Room.

Isaac and I chased after her and were closing in when all at once she turned around, screaming, "Aaaaaahhhh," and came flying our way.

"What's wrong?" Isaac cried, reeling backward.

"Over there!" she screamed, pointing behind her as she tore by. "A zombie! In a wheelchair!"

Our jaws went danglin'.

A zombie in a wheelchair?

Isaac and I watched her go, then cocked eyebrows at each other. Neither of us had to say it, 'cause there are just some things you have to see for yourself.

We weren't takin' chances, though. No, sir! We moved like sneak thieves up the walkway, our eyes peeled. "You believe in zombies?" I whispered.

"Nah. You?"

"Nah."

Then we saw it.

"Aaaah!" we both cried, coming together like magnets.

We watched it sitting there, in a wheelchair between shrubs, white as moonlight, twitching.

"What is it?" Isaac breathed.

It still wasn't jumping up to get us, so I stepped in closer. "It's only a mannequin," I whispered over my shoulder. "They use 'em for training."

"Why's it in the bushes? And why's it *moving*?"

"Maybe they wanted to hide it from folks 'cause they couldn't get it to stop twitchin'?"

"Maybe they should just disconnect the circuitry?"

"Maybe they didn't know how? Or ran out of time?" I shrugged. "They've been workin' hard all day to make everything perfect."

That seemed to snap loose circuits together in Isaac's mind. "We have *got* to get inside." He looked back the way we'd come and shouted, "Liza!" then took off, saying, "We're going to be in so much trouble!"

"Come back this way when you find her!" I called after him. "I'll get someone to let us in!"

"Right!"

Racing to the back door of the Activities Room, I passed by a big window and looked inside. Mr. Freize was talking, and Purple Shirts were lined up on either side of him. Ma was on the very end, looking around.

Looking for me.

I keyed in the code quick, opened the door, and slipped in a rock to keep it from closing again. Then I raced back to find Isaac and Liza. "Over here!" I called when I saw them coming. "They let me in!"

I flicked the rock out of the way without them noticing, and we made our way back to our seats, trying to be as smooth as possible—which wasn't that smooth, seein' how the director was making a speech and everyone else was quiet and listening.

Mrs. Monroe rolled her eyes as we settled in, but she seemed more relieved than mad, since the dark look Liza had been wearing before was gone.

After a minute had passed and Isaac knew he was off the hook, he nudged me under the table and mouthed, "Zombie in a wheelchair!"

I did my best to keep from laughing, but it was hard.

42

Yellow as Jell-O

I was still grinnin' like a fool about the zombie in a wheelchair when I heard Mr. Freize say Ma's name. And right after, the whole room broke out in applause. Big applause. Like my ma was the winner of some important award.

Was I missing something?

A few folks stood up, still clapping, and then more folks stood up. Pretty soon all the families were standing up, clapping. I looked around in wonder, then gave Isaac a little shrug and stood up, too.

When folks started sitting again, the director laughed and said, "I was going to suggest you give our team a round of applause, but I can see that you already understand what an incredible job they do. So this seems like a good time to remind you that our caregiver Christmas donation box is in the foyer. In the spirit of giving and thanks, remember to give generously!" He picked up a glass and lifted it. "Thank you for coming tonight. Thank you for trusting us with your loved ones. Now please enjoy our Brookside Thanksgiving."

So all the clapping and cheering wasn't just for Ma. But it was *partly* for Ma, which still left me feeling partly stunned. And then Isaac's ma leaned over and caught my eye. "You have no idea how much I appreciate your mother. She's an angel, she really is."

Ma? An *angel*?

Guess she'd never seen Ma draggin' home after work. Or been hollered at by her for running late. Or been cuffed for sassing.

I was still wrapping my head around all the standing and clapping and folks thinking Ma was an angel when food started appearing in front of me. First a little plate of salad slid in. Then metal tongs came over my shoulder and left a roll on another little plate. Then a big plate with a turkey slice and mashed potatoes and marshmallow yams and green beans got delivered. It all happened so fast that I was still busy with one thing when the next showed up.

"They *are* efficient," Mrs. Monroe said with a smile.

I guess most folks were busy trying to keep up with the deliveries, 'cause there was more clinking of dishes than talking going on. You could even hear the background music. It was the fancy kind, with violins and horns and cellos and stuff.

And I was just thinking how the horns sounded like someone was playing them into a pillow when a voice broke through like reveille, shouting, "Stop that!"

I looked over in time to see Sir Robert fling the water from his glass at Teddy C. Teddy got hit, but not as bad as Pom-Pom Pam, who got a big, wet splat on the side of her hair.

Teddy C looked stunned, but Pam was up like a shot.

Like she was back on the field, cheering again.

Only she wasn't cheering.

She was flinging mashed potatoes, shouting, "You ruined my hair!"

I'm pretty sure she was aiming at Sir Robert, but her throwing arm was probably not in practice, 'cause she missed by a mile and hit Alice instead.

Alice didn't waste time calling her sweet pea. She broke into language so nasty she'd have been suspended from school for life. And with her words came food, flingin' through the air. Potatoes. Rolls. Green beans. Yams. She threw everything she could scoop up but still couldn't seem to hit Pam. She hit everyone around *but* Pam.

Then the volcano erupted. The oldies who'd been hit started hurling food and insults.

"Take that, you wrinkled prune!"

"Who you callin' wrinkled?"

"You, you ugly, shriveled pile of wrinkles!"

"If I'm a prune, you're a . . . a big, fat *cauliflower*!"

"Prunes?" Debbie Rucker called. "I love prunes! Can I have some?"

But while Debbie was asking for prunes, the rest of the room was going nuts.

"Stop stealin' my food!"

"It's my food!"

"I need seconds! Someone bring me seconds!"

"He means ammo! Don't bring him anything!"

And all the while, food was flying.

"Who did that?" someone screamed. "Who hit me? You?"

"No! It was her!"

"Liar! I'll sue!"

"I'll sue you for calling me a liar!"

"Prunes!" Debbie shouted. "I want prunes!"

Mashed potatoes thumped against my head. Isaac saw and said, "This is crazy!"

I peeled the mush out of my hair. "Reminds me of ridin' the school bus."

"Yeah, right?" Isaac laughed.

"You ride the bus?" I asked, still peelin' out mush.

"The thirty-three. Hate it."

"I'm on the twenty-seven. Hate it worse!"

Ruby had been quiet until then, but she perked up now and started ripping at her blouse, singing at the top of her lungs, *"Just a spoonful of sugar helps the medicine go down!"*

"Mother!" Mrs. Monroe cried. "What are you doing?"

Buttons were poppin' all over the place. *"Medicine go down . . ."*

"Mother!"

"Medicine go down!"

"Mother, stop that!"

"Just a spoonful of sugar—"

"MOTHER!"

While Mrs. Monroe tried putting Ruby's clothes back together, Sir Robert—who was wiping food off his face with his neck scarf—shouted, "You're as yellow as Jell-O!" at Teddy C.

"Jell-O?" Debbie hollered. *"I* want Jell-O!"

Food stopped flying.

There was a murmur of "Is there Jell-O?" and then the place went quiet.

All the oldies looked around.

"Can we have Jell-O?" Debbie asked.

All eyes turned to the director. His suit was spotted with potatoes. His face was twisted in terror.

"Sure," Gloria said, taking charge. "I think we have some in the kitchen." She gave a stern look around the tables. "But you have to behave. If you can't behave, you can't have Jell-O. Do we have a deal?"

All the oldies nodded.

The families let out huge sighs of relief.

And just like that, the food fight was over.

(43)

Leftovers

Ma got off work even later than expected. *"Lord,"* she said, collapsin' into a window seat on the bus ride home. "I am worn clear down to the bone."

She settled in, with her bag on her lap and a care package of leftovers at her feet. The director had forced monster-sized helpings of food on any of the day-shifters who'd stayed late to clean up. They were packed in plastic containers and put inside big cloth bags.

I wasn't sure what-all was in ours.

I was praying there was no zombie turkey.

Ma might have been worn clear down to the bone, but her mouth sure wasn't actin' like it. The minute she sat down, it started flappin' away, forgettin' all about her fancy *g*'s.

"All that work we did makin' sure everything was perfect?" she moaned. "Why'd we bother? It was like bein' in a room with two-year-olds." She gave a little snort. "That's what everyone says, right? They become children again. They squall and cry and demand and fight. And I've seen 'em swipe food, or spit it back out, but *Lord*, an actual food fight? And the families just *sat* there."

"It was pretty crazy," I offered.

"Yes," she said, turning to face me square-on. "Yes, it was. There is no other word to describe it. You can say it again."

"Ma'am?"

"It's okay. Say it again."

"Crazy?"

"Yes. That is the one and only word for tonight. Crazy."

I laughed. "And here I was tryin' to quit sayin' it."

She laughed, too, then heaved a big sigh and went quiet. I just sat watching the wheels turn in her head, until finally what she was thinking began slipping out. "Today was hard the whole way around." She slid a look my way. "Except for one thing."

I thought back, trying to figure what that might be. It had been a long one, that's for sure, from Mrs. White dying to cleaning up after a food fight.

"You and Isaac," she said, saving me from recalling the details.

"Me and Isaac?"

"Mm-hmm. It was so nice to see you *playin'* with someone."

"We weren't *playin'*."

"Maybe I was readin' those happy cheeks wrong?"

"What happy cheeks?"

"The ones you were wearing when you came sneakin' in from whatever mischief you two were up to outside."

I tried to wipe the *uh-oh* from my face.

She laughed, and for all the weight of tired I knew she was carrying right then, that laugh lifted her like an invisible balloon. "Doesn't matter, and I don't care. I just liked seein' the two of you havin' a good time."

"I thought you might be mad about us comin' in when the director was talking."

She gave me a sweet smile. "He was just doin' the introductions. It was a good part to miss."

"It got you a standing ovation, though. That was nice, right?"

"Yes, it was," she said. And after a minute, she added, "It's nice to be appreciated."

I could see her driftin' off in her mind again, and when she came back, she said, "I wish there was a way folks could know what it's like without actually livin' through it."

"You mean bein' . . . havin' . . ."

"Alzheimer's. Dementia. It's hard. It's hard any way you look at it. For them, for the families, for us." She let out a heavy sigh. "You try to give folks dignity to the end, but you lose your own along the way."

"What do you mean?"

She gave me a never-mind shake of the head.

"Ma?"

She tested me with a good, long stare, then said, "I change diapers, Lincoln. Big, messy diapers. It's not in a world anywhere near glamorous."

"You do a lot more than change diapers!" It came out a whisper.

This time her smile was small and sad. "I know, but none of it erases the diaper changin', now does it?"

I kept on whisperin'. "Isaac's ma said she thinks you're an angel."

"That's nice. . . ." Her voice trailed off, and I could see her mind leapfroggin' from one tired place to another.

"Ma?"

"Hmm?"

"What are you thinkin'?"

"Oh, just that Isaac's ma's an interior designer."

"A what?"

"She styles folks' homes."

"How do you style a home? What does that mean? And why you thinkin' about that?"

She shook her head. "Never mind."

"But . . . what does it have to do with her callin' you an angel?"

She turned to me, and her face seemed so . . . pained.

"Ma? What's wrong?"

She stayed quiet, and her eyes were holding mine like she was waiting for *me* to say something.

"Ma?" I said again. "Tell me."

Her head wobbled again as her eyes broke away.

Then she leaned against the window and stayed that way for the rest of the ride home.

(44)

Shot of Knowledge

The second time I woke up the next day, it was from knowing what I should have said to Ma on the bus.

It rang through my head like a shot in the woods.

I wanted to race downstairs and call her from the pay phone, but she'd made me promise something when she'd woken me up earlier. "You can stay here today," she'd whispered, "if you swear you won't go downstairs."

"Huh?" It was dark and cold in the apartment. It felt like the middle of the night.

"I have to catch the bus. Now swear it, unless you want me draggin' you along."

She was leavin' for work? How could it be time to leave already? My whole body felt sore from the day before. Sore and tired. Like I needed to sleep for days.

"Swear," she whispered louder. "Swear or get your shoes on this instant."

"I swear," I said, and I meant it.

All two words of it.

Then I went back to sleep and stayed that way for another four hours, which is when I woke up with the shot of knowledge ringing through my head.

I stumbled to the kitchen sink for a drink of water, and after slurpin' upside down at the faucet, I found a note on the table. A note outlining things I was to do and not do.

Nowhere on the *Don't* list was *sleep all day,* so I fell back into bed, thinking that at least I wasn't breaking any rules. And then I just lay there, wishing I could go downstairs and call Ma.

I needed to tell her what I should have said on the bus.

After frettin' about it for a while, I decided I'd write her a note. I'd get the words just right and hand them to her when she got home. But try as I might, I couldn't get the words even close to right. I went through page after page trying, but it kept coming out wrong. How could I write whole stories but not a little note?

Finally I gave it a rest and tended to the list Ma had made. I wiped down the counter, swept the floors, scrubbed the toilet, cleaned the mirror, and picked up around the place.

Then I ate a peanut butter sandwich and got caught up in thinkin' about Ma.

Why was I so bad at *saying* this?

Maybe I was using too many words.

Maybe I should make her a list instead.

Yeah, a list!

So I got busy with that, only to discover it made what I was trying to say doubly dorky.

So I ripped it up, too, and went back to Ma's list.

Fix Carol Graves a plate and take it to her popped out at me. I figured chances were slim to none that Carol Graves would answer the door, so I didn't get fancy fixin' the plate. I just shoveled some Brookside Thanksgiving leftovers on and took it over.

I knocked on the door, *bang, bang, bang,* holding the plate away so no flakes of paint landed in the food.

I waited, then put my ear up to the door, wondering if I'd get a peek at One-Eyed Jack. Just the thought made my heart speed up. Made me remember—One-Eyed Jack might be telepathic!

So I tried again, *bang, bang, bang,* and this time when I listened, I could hear coughing. A slow, grinding kind of cough. Like someone tryin' to turn over a motor when the battery's about dead.

I knocked again and was fixin' to call out, "Just deliverin' Thanksgiving supper!" but changed my mind as the words were set to launch. "Delivery from Shop-Wise Grocers!" I called. "Need you to sign!"

It came out sounding all leprechaun-y, too.

My ear told me the coughing was getting closer. Very slowly closer. I also heard, "Coming," but it was feeble as could be. Nothing admiral-y about it.

When the door finally opened, Mrs. Graves was panting hard and didn't even seem to care that she'd been tricked. I was expecting to have to do some fancy talking, or even stick my foot in to keep the door from slamming in my face, but she took one look at me and started shuf- flin' back the way she'd come, still coughing.

"I brought you a Thanksgiving meal," I said, following her to her sunny spot by the window. The Mirror Cats were coming out to see me, mewing like they wanted the food themselves. I looked around for Jack but didn't see him. "You want me to heat it up?" I asked.

She was in her seat now, coughing away. I waited for an answer, but I think it was too hard for her to cough and nod.

There were lots of cups and mugs on the coffee table near her, and thinking that one might have something she could drink to help with the coughing, I checked them over and saw mold floating inside them.

I raced to the kitchen and fetched some fresh water from the tap. When I delivered it to her, she was too shaky to hold the cup herself, so I held it up for her and let her sip until she pushed it away.

"Are you okay?" I asked, though it was pretty easy to see she wasn't.

She nodded. "Take Jack home with you."

Her voice was so little I could barely hear her, and I was sure I'd heard her wrong. "Ma'am?"

"Jack. Take him home. The others will kill him."

Kill him?

The Mirror Cats were right there beside us, meowing and flicking their tails, but I still didn't see Jack.

"Where is he?"

"Hiding. Promise me you'll take him."

I nodded. "Are they hungry?" I asked, watching the Mirror Cats.

"They have food."

"How about you?" I took in all the dishes beside her. Most were scary gross with mold. "I'll heat up the food I brought."

She nodded like she barely cared and closed her eyes.

I went to the kitchen, keeping my eyes peeled for Jack. "Here, kitty," I called, but that just brought the Mirror Cats closer, mewing at my feet.

I took the plate I'd brought, put it inside the microwave that was buried in the corner of her counter, and set the timer at only one minute. I'd learned from Gloria that old-ies like their food warm, but barely. If you heat it so *you* think it's just right, they'll scream that their mouth is on fire.

Or spit it back at you.

While the microwave was going, I checked the cat zone and found that the food-and-water tower was knocked over. The Mirror Cats were right there, crying, so I set the tower up and got it working again. "There you go," I told them, and when they pounced in to eat, I took up calling for Jack. "Here, kitty, kitty."

I couldn't find him anywhere, so I went back to the microwave, and as I was pulling out the plate, I felt him standing alongside me.

He wasn't touching me, I just knew he was there.

"Hey, fella," I said, stooping down with a piece of turkey in my hand. He had claw marks scabbed across his muzzle and some newer blood on his side. "Here you go, boy," I said, tearing off little pieces of turkey and placing them on the floor.

When he'd finished, I took him and the plate over to Mrs. Graves, along with a cup of juice. She was sound asleep, and every breath she took gurgled. Her lips were cracked and her eyes looked crusted. It was like she was drowning and drying out, all at the same time.

"Ma'am?" I said, sitting in a chair beside her. "You need to eat something." When she didn't answer, I nudged her. "Ma'am? Please. At least have some juice."

"Just leave it," she whispered. "I'll be fine."

I watched her falling back to sleep and nudged her again. "Ma'am? I think I should get you to the hospital."

"No," she gurgled. "Just leave me here in the sun. It's what I want." She opened her eyes to see Jack sitting on my lap. "But take him with you. He deserves someone like you. Take anything you need. There's food."

"Can *you* try to eat?" I begged. "Just a bite or two?"

She shook her head. "Maybe in a little while." She closed her eyes, and the wrinkles on her face smoothed away. "Come back then."

She was falling asleep again, so I stood and said, "I will."

Then I tucked a blanket over her and leaned in, whispering, "Sweet dreams."

45

Not Alone

By the time Ma came home from work, I had a lot of explaining to do. There was a litter box in the bathroom, kibble in the kitchen, and a one-eyed cat roaming around.

Ma took it all in as she unloaded from work. "Lincoln Jones, you have a lot of explaining to do."

"Yes, ma'am. I know."

"So . . . ?"

There was one thing I wanted to clear up right off the bat. "I did not go downstairs. Everything's from next door."

"And . . . ?"

"And I only went next door 'cause it was on your list."

"And . . . ?"

"And before I tell you about that, there's something else I want to tell you."

She was sitting now, at the table that I'd set for dinner, with the chair turned out to face me. Her arms were movin' into the crisscross position that meant she was holdin' back from sayin' what she was thinking. "Well . . . ?" she demanded.

"I'm sorry I didn't say it on the bus last night. And I'm sorry I couldn't figure out how to say it on paper. I tried, and I tried hard, but it just sounded stupid."

"Lincoln, what *are* you getting at?"

And that's when the jumble of words came tumbling out. "You get up in the dark and don't come home 'til after dark. You work all day at makin' other folks comfortable and dignified, which leaves you tired to the bone and feelin' undignified. And I know the reason you work so hard isn't just to give oldies dignity. It's 'cause of me. 'Cause you want me to have a life where I'm safe and don't have to hide under the bed. And if that means changin' big ol' messy diapers, that's what you're willing to do."

Ma's eyes were startin' to run, so I took in a deep breath and got to what I was really wanting to say. "What I should have said last night was that I'm *proud* of you. I think you're a wonder. I wouldn't trade you for anyone's ma. Not anyone's!" Her eyes were spillin' over now, so while she was reaching for a napkin to dry her face, I finished up quick. "And I don't want to live someplace that's been styled. I like it here. It's styled just fine the way it is."

Ma wiped her face and blew her nose and sniffed. Then

she gave me a look that was one hundred percent suspicious. "Is this your way of buttering me up about the cat?"

"No!"

She laughed and sniffed some more and put her arms out. And when I came in for a hug, she whispered, "I would have said yes anyway."

"Ma!"

She laughed again. "Now tell me what happened. How'd we get a cat?"

So I told her about Mrs. Graves and the Mirror Cats attacking Jack and how I'd been going back every hour all afternoon to check on things next door. "She doesn't want me to call anyone, and she doesn't want to go to the hospital. I think she just wants to die, Ma, right there in her sunny window."

"What if a doctor could help her?"

"She told me a hundred times to let her go in peace."

Ma was quiet for a long time, staring at the floor, her head shaking back and forth from time to time. Finally, she heaved a sigh and said, "Take me there?"

So I did, and after Ma checked Mrs. Graves over, she pulled a chair right alongside her and held her hand. "You can go home, Lincoln, but I need to stay here," she said. "So she knows she's not alone."

"I think she wants to be alone, Ma."

Ma looked at me with a smile that was three parts sad and seven parts wise. "No one wants to be alone, especially now."

"But she's sleepin'," I whispered. "She's been sleepin' all afternoon. She doesn't even know we're here."

"Oh, she knows, Lincoln." Her face was now all parts wise. "She knows."

So I pulled up a chair alongside, too. I didn't know how long I could take just sitting there, but I did know one thing.

I didn't want Ma to be alone, either.

46

Freedom

Mrs. Graves passed during the night. I was asleep in the chair when Ma shook me awake and whispered, "She's gone, Lincoln. Let's get home."

I was still half in a dream where I was trying to leave a strange room but the door going out took me right back inside the very same room. I kept going round and round and round, not knowing how to get out.

And now I was wakin' up in a strange room with a dead body in it.

I was feeling mighty bamboozled.

"What are we supposed to do now?" I asked.

"Shh."

Didn't seem like much of an answer to me. And I wasn't sure why we were bein' quiet, or why tiptoein' was in order.

It wasn't like we were going to wake her up. But I was too tired to put up a fuss and more'n happy to go. I followed Ma out the door, glad it didn't take me back inside the very same room.

When we were in our own apartment, I went straight for my mattress. And I was half asleep and half wishing for an extra blanket when Ma came over and whispered, "I'll be back. I need to make a few calls."

I don't know how long she was gone, but when she slipped back in, I thought I was dreaming, 'cause there was a cat curled up at my chest, purring.

And then I remembered—I had a cat!

"Ma?"

"Shh. Everything's fine."

The purring at my chest made me believe it was so.

Ma did not take pity on me in the morning. "You're coming with me," she said soon after her alarm went off.

"But, Ma!"

"Don't fuss. You're comin'."

"What about Mrs. Graves?"

"They came and got her last night."

"Who did?"

"The coroner's office. You didn't hear?"

"No!"

"Well, they did. Now get movin'."

"But, Ma!"

"Get movin'!"

On the bus ride to Brookside, I noticed the dark bags under Ma's eyes, but she wasn't lettin' on how little sleep she'd had, if she'd had any at all. She told me that the Mirror Cats would be fine and that everything else would be taken care of without us. "Families have responsibilities, whether they like it or not."

"She had family?"

"I told you she did."

"But . . . who are they?"

"Two feuding sons. One's in Florida, the other's in Los Angeles."

"How do you know?"

"I found a letter and instructions in a drawer."

"You went nosin' through her stuff?"

"Mm-hmm," she said.

It was a highfalutin *mm-hmm,* too. One that said loud and clear that I'd best not be passing judgment.

Still, I couldn't help thinking about it. How could someone have two kids and wind up dyin' with strangers? What were her sons like? Why were they feuding? Did they know where she was living? Did they know *how* she was living? Did they know their ma had lost track of what was garbage and what wasn't?

Did they know she needed help?

At Brookside, I tried escapin' into my notebook. Into a story. I had to be at Brookside all day, and I just wanted to block it out. Before, I could always do that with writing stories, but now I couldn't seem to get into one. I couldn't tune out bein' there. And bein' there felt like it was sucking the life right out of me.

"You doing okay today, dear?" Gloria asked me after lunch. "Your mother told me about what happened. You've had quite a couple of days, haven't you?"

I just nodded and told her I was fine. But I felt strange. Like something inside me had changed.

Ma seemed to have changed, too, but in a different way. "I got a raise!" she whispered on the bus ride home.

"Really?"

"A good one! It came with a glowing review from the director, too. He said he likes my work ethic and my patience with the residents. He told me he always hears good things about me and that he's grateful for the way I stepped up during Thanksgiving. He also noticed the way you pitched in and told me I'm raising a fine young man."

"He said that?"

She gave me a look that was all parts mischief. "Well, he doesn't know about you callin' folks crazies or forcing garlic on me to fight off psychic vampires."

"I didn't force garlic on you! And I sure didn't tell you to *peel* it!"

She laughed. A big, smiley, cheek-poppin' laugh. I hadn't seen her this happy in . . . ever.

"You know what this is?" she asked, wagging a Brookside envelope with her paycheck in it.

"A Brookside envelope with your paycheck in it?" I ventured.

"It's more than that. It's freedom. Tomorrow I'll send

Ellie what I owe her, plus some thank-you money, and then I can start savin' for *us*."

"Uh . . . can the thank-you money and the savin' maybe wait 'til after Christmas?"

She turned a cool look on me. "What? Getting a cat's not enough?"

My face flashed wide, but it came back in quick. The truth is, if she'd have asked me what my wildest dreams would bring me for Christmas, I'd have said a cat. Jack had just arrived early, is all.

She laughed at my face flashing around and said, "We'll have a fine Christmas, Lincoln. I promise. And next year? What do you say we start looking for an apartment with heat in it?"

"That would be nice," I agreed.

"Mighty nice," she said, and she smiled the whole way home.

47

Brave

The best thing about what was left of Thanksgiving break was Jack. He was like my new shadow, followin' me everywhere I went. And when I sat down or rested on my bed, he'd curl up right there with me. I spent a whole lot of the weekend talking to Jack.

I also spent a whole lot of the weekend wishing Jack could talk to me. I had questions! Had Mrs. Graves taken him in after he'd become One-Eyed Jack? Or had the Mirror Cats slashed his eye? I wished he could tell me.

The worst thing about the weekend was not the shopping or the chores. It was Sunday morning, when it was just Jack and me in the apartment and Ma was at work. I almost wished she'd made me go to Brookside with her.

It wasn't just being trapped by my promise to stay

inside the apartment. It was everything that was going on outside the apartment. I guess they wanted to clear Mrs. Graves's place out quick, 'cause even though it was Sunday, workers were walking back and forth, back and forth, emptying out the apartment. I spied on them through the window blinds, careful not to let on that I was home. Someone figuring out I was home was the first step in them knowing I was home alone.

The workers did carry out some boxes of stuff, but mostly what they hauled away were black trash bags, stuffed full and round. One after the other after the other. It was like an army of big black ants marching past, working in a line.

I wondered about Mrs. Graves's feuding sons. Where were they? The men cleaning out the apartment were hired workers. I could tell by their boots and shirts and the way they marched along and worked together. This was a job. They didn't care about anything else.

So why weren't the sons here? Didn't *they* care?

I also wondered about all the stuff Mrs. Graves had saved, thinking she might need it someday. Toothbrushes, toilet-paper rolls, butter tubs, bread bags . . . it was all being hauled off to the dump. She treated it like treasure, but to everyone else it was just trash.

It all felt sad. And it lingered in my mind long after the army had stopped marching. I couldn't figure out answers for any of it, and after Ma was finally home, she was no help at all. "Hoarding's a common problem with seniors, and folks have fallings-out, Lincoln. You can't solve all the world's problems. You gotta start by fixin' your own."

Seemed kinda funny coming from someone who'd delivered zombie chicken to a homeless guy and sat up all night with a dying stranger. And what had Ma meant about "fixin' your own"?

I was almost asleep when I remembered how Ma had called her sister to patch things up. She could have just left things as they were, but she'd called Ellie and tried to make them better. I lay there in the dark, figuring out, finally, how important that was.

Then my mind started rewinding. Working backward in time, thinking about all the things that had happened since Ma had made her resolution on New Year's almost a year ago.

I always knew Ma worked hard. And I knew she'd made a plan and was sticking to it. As tough as everything was, she was sticking to it.

But there was something else. Something I hadn't known before. And right there, in the dark, it clicked. More than any of the heroes in my stories, more than any other person I'd ever known, Ma was brave.

Truly brave.

And seein' that clear as day right through the dark made me know something else. It had come and gone in little waves before, but it was settling now, way down inside.

I could be brave, too.

48

Surprises

Isaac was waiting for me when I got off the bus Monday morning. "Hey!" he called.

His hair was combed back and still a little wet. I went over to him, thinking that instead of a wild anemone mule, he looked like a turtle walking on two legs. "What's in there?" I asked, slapping his backpack.

"Oh, everything!"

He sounded mighty excited, and it made me laugh. I slipped him a wily look. "Like . . . a zombie in a wheelchair?"

He laughed, too. "Wish I'd known you were going to be at Brookside on Friday," he said. "I'd have come."

"To Brookside?" My face went a little screwy. "Why? And how'd you know I was there?"

"My mom. She said she saw you looking all miserable in a corner."

"She did?" I thought back to Friday. It *had* been a long and miserable day. One that would have been a whole lot better with Isaac there. "It was the slowest day ever. . . ."

"No food fights?"

I laughed again. "Dentures went flyin', but that's about it."

"Hey, are you doing the Alzheimer's Walk on Saturday?"

"Uh . . . I don't think so. It's Ma's only real day off."

"Well, my mom said if you wanted, you could come home with me Friday after school and we could camp out in the tree fort and then do the walk on Saturday."

My mind went twirlin'. "You have a tree fort?"

"Yeah! It's got a trapdoor, a pulley-system dumbwaiter, and a telescope for stars."

I was in. I was all in. "I need to ask Ma, but . . . sure!"

The warning bell rang. "Hey," he said, "you want to meet up at lunch?"

I laughed. "For a food fight?"

He smiled, big and bright. "I'm up for that!"

"Maybe they're servin' Jell-O!"

He laughed, too, then said, "What do you do at recess?"

I shrugged, not wantin' to say I hid out somewhere with my notebook.

"I could meet you right here if you want. We could hang out?"

For the first time since school started, I was bubblin'

inside. Bubblin' with the excitement of findin' a friend. "Sure!"

Then Kandi came running up. Her cheeks were all rosy, and her fingernails were painted white with red stripes. Like candy canes. She probably thought she was being clever, but I thought it was annoying. December was still a day away, and she was already claimin' it as *her* month.

She looked back and forth between Isaac and me with nosy written all over her face. "So . . . did you have a nice Thanksgiving?"

I slid a look at Isaac.

He slid a look at me.

"It was fine," I said, and Isaac nodded his agreement.

"I didn't know you two were friends," she said, and she was twitchin' a little. Like she was feeling guilty for what she'd said about Isaac.

"Uh-huh," I said, giving her a cool look.

"I'm glad," she said, still twitching. And since we weren't saying anything more, she ran off, calling, "We need to get to class!"

"Her mother died last year," Isaac said, watching her go.

"What?" I wasn't even sure he'd actually said it. It was so out of the blue.

"Brain cancer. It happened quick."

"What?" I still wasn't sure this was a real conversation.

"My sister says she's a mess."

"Your sister does?"

"Yeah. She knows her sister."

"Whose sister?"

"Kandi's sister."

"Kandi has a sister?" I said it like it was the world's biggest revelation. I have no idea why.

Isaac laughed. "A lot of people do."

The blacktop was almost cleared, and we were going to be late, so we took off running. "I'll meet you at recess!" I called.

"Righty-o!" he called back.

In class, Kandi was being chatty with everyone around her. She sure didn't seem messed up to me. She seemed nosy. And annoying. And seeing her flit around, smiling all the time . . . seeing her boss folks like a camp director . . . seeing her throw little tantrums when things didn't go her way . . . none of it added up to her being messed up. It added up to her being kinda *spoiled*.

But maybe I'd added things up wrong.

It felt like when I'd read the Resident Spotlights in the *Brookside Bulletin*. I'd thought I had folks all figured out, then it turned out I didn't know much about them at all. But it was more than that. All this time I'd been writing stories about made-up people that I could see clear as day, but the real folks around me had stories I'd been completely blind to.

The thought put me in a wobbly mood. Ms. Miller, though, was in a great mood, and very excited about our new writing assignment. "You're going to detail your

Thanksgiving experience," she said, pacing around like a caged tiger. "I want you to use all the senses. What you saw, what you heard, what you smelled, what you tasted. . . . Make me feel like I was there."

Colby's hand shot up, and when Ms. Miller called on her, Colby asked, "So you want us to describe Thanksgiving dinner?"

"You don't have to limit yourself to dinner. The buildup to dinner, the cleanup after dinner, the family traditions, the games you played or movies you watched. Did you travel? What was that like? How about Black Friday? Did you go shopping?" She laughed, like she was going back in her mind, remembering. "Lots of sights and sounds there!"

Benny called out, "How long does it have to be?"

"This is a volume piece. The longer the better," she said. "Grab me with your opening line and go! I will not be grading on syntax. I want you just to write, write, write. I want you to *enjoy* the process and not worry about anything but getting your experience down on paper."

"So how many pages for an A?" Colby asked.

"Hmm," she said, studying her. "How about ten? Yes, ten!"

She was winging it like no teacher I'd ever known.

"Ten?!" Benny cried. "I can't write ten pages!"

"Then maybe you'll only write seven and get a C." She leveled a look at the class. "You had five days off. Tell me about them."

Back before Thanksgiving break, I could have written ten pages about any made-up story, easy. Which means that before Thanksgiving break, I could have *made up* a story of what happened on my Thanksgiving break, easy. Like, I could have made up a story about Aunt Ellie and Cheyenne coming over to our big house for a feast. Wild turkeys could have been flappin' and gobble-gobblin' in the backyard tree, tryin' to escape their doom. Our dog—a big, happy hound—could have been barking and bounding around all over the place, trying to reach the turkeys. I could have planted our own garden in the story, where corn and yams and carrots were just waitin' to be harvested.

I could have, and who would've known it wasn't true?

Nobody.

And nobody would've cared.

But now I felt strange inside. Like I was done with making stuff up. Done running from things. Done hiding.

But I couldn't write about what *had* happened. If I told the truth, Ms. Miller might call the cops. Besides, how could I explain how I'd spent most of my vacation with folks who had lost their minds? How I'd seen two old ladies die? How I'd eaten leftovers from a food-fight Thanksgiving meal for four days running and had hidden out from an army of ants in an apartment with my new, one-eyed cat?

There was no explaining it. Not in ten pages, not in a hundred.

So while Colby's feather pencil flapped around and Rayne and Wynne had their noses low over their pages and scribbled away, I sat on the edge of our continent with a blank page, feeling stuck.

Stuck and alone.

49

I Do Declare

After that first half hour of writing, we had a math lesson, and then we were back to writing again 'cause Colby raised her feather and begged, "Can we have more time on our essay? Please?"

I'm guessin' she'd had a Thanksgiving worth writing about.

I watched her feather do the mad flap for a while, and then I guess I was staring at Rayne's paper, 'cause she asked, "Why aren't you writing?"

I hunkered down, shielding my blank page after that. And I *tried* to come up with something, but I was tangled up inside. All I had for my essay when the recess bell rang was a title: "My Thanksgiving."

When Ms. Miller released us, I busted out of the room

and cut across the blacktop toward where Isaac said he'd meet me. I was hoping his class had to write a Thanksgiving essay. I thought maybe he could help me figure out what to do.

I was almost at the spot when Troy Pilkers stepped in my way. "I do declare!" he said. "If it ain't the Missing Link."

He was making fun of me being from the South.

He was also baiting me.

I didn't bite, but my heart was beating fast as I tried sidestepping him.

He sidestepped, too. "Whassamatter, sugar? Cat got your tongue?"

I tried sidestepping again, but when he blocked me again, I squared up and said, "It's not my fault you got thrown off the bus."

"Well, shut my mouth! If that don't put pepper in the gumbo!"

"*What?*" I gave him a good, hard squint. "That makes no sense."

He dropped the Southern thing. "Yeah? So who was it?" He shoved me. "Who got me thrown off?"

The shove wasn't that hard, but it set something off in me. I wanted to run. Find a corner somewhere and wait for it to be over.

But my feet stayed planted, and I drilled him with a look that said he was dumber'n dirt. "*You* did. Driver's got a mirror, you know."

Before Troy could answer, Isaac stepped in. "Hey! Why'd you shove him?"

Troy zeroed in on him. "You really taking me on, Dweebly?"

Out of nowhere, Kandi was there, too, with a four-square ball tucked under her arm. "Oh, grow up, Troy."

Troy took in the three of us, then stared at her. "These two? Seriously?"

"You don't know anything about them, okay? Maybe if you did, you wouldn't be so mean."

"I was just goofing around," he said with a shrug. "He could have asked me to stop, you know."

I stretched up an extra inch. "Like you need to be asked to quit flingin' tuna in someone's hair?"

"Yeah," Kandi said. "Only an idiot would need to be told that's not cool." And then she did the most surprising thing I'd ever seen at school. She softened her voice like Gloria always does to calm down the oldies and said, "I don't think you're an idiot, Troy. So just be nice, would you? It's not hard."

He stared at her some more, then grumbled, "Whatever," and walked away.

"Wow," I said, watching him go.

Isaac nodded. "That was unexpected."

Kandi smiled at us, then looked out at the four-square court, where kids were waiting for her to return with the ball. "You guys want to play?"

"I'm terrible," Isaac said, shaking his head.

"Me too."

Kandi punched her free hand to her side. "Oh, just come, would you? Everyone's terrible. It doesn't matter. It's just fun."

I looked at Isaac and shrugged.

He shrugged back.

And we followed Kandi to the four-square court.

50

Opening Up

Trouble was waiting for me inside the classroom. During recess, Ms. Miller had gone around to each desk and looked over our essays. "Lincoln," she said, and wagged a finger for me to follow her outside.

As quiet as she'd said it, the whole class knew I was in trouble. And as hard as they tried, their sly-eye watching me go was nowhere near sly.

"I thought you loved to write," Ms. Miller said when the door was closed.

I stared at my shoes.

"Lincoln? Look at me."

I looked up, then went back to my shoes.

"Lincoln, you can write about anything. Anything that happened over Thanksgiving break. It doesn't have to be about the dinner."

I nodded.

"Lincoln?"

"Yes, ma'am."

"Do you celebrate Thanksgiving?"

I nodded, which seemed to send relief streakin' through her.

"Well, then, what's the problem? I thought you would love this assignment! You are my very best writer, did you know that?"

I shook my head.

"You have a wonderful way with words. I always look forward to reading your essays."

"Thank you, ma'am."

She stood lookin' at me for an endless minute. Finally she said, "Is everything all right at home?"

I nodded.

"Lincoln?"

She had a look on her face that was all parts doubt, and it set a wave of panic crashing through me. "No!" I said, lookin' straight at her. "Things at home are *fine*. They're great. Actually, they've never been better!"

"So . . . ?"

I shrugged and went back to looking down. "So there's no explainin' the Thanksgiving I had."

She shook her head. "I don't understand this. You love to write, everything at home is fine, you celebrate Thanksgiving—"

"Well, I don't know if you'd call it *celebratin*'."

She gave me a curious look. "So what *would* you call it?"

I thought about that. "Surviving? I survived it?" Then, under my breath, I added, "Which is more'n I can say about some folks."

She crossed her arms. "Okay. Now I am completely confused."

"I know, ma'am, see?"

"No! I don't see!"

"Exactly! There's no explainin' it."

"Well." She studied me hard while I did the same to my shoes. Finally she said, "How can anyone understand if you don't at least try to explain?" Then she softened up and said, "I know you're new here, and I know that's not easy. I have no idea what you're going through or why your vacation was . . . difficult. But I can see that you have a story to tell, and your story *matters*."

I peeked up at her.

"I promise you, Lincoln, it matters." She gave me a little smile. "Can you please just try?"

"I have tried, ma'am. I don't know how to start."

My not knowing how to start seemed to make her very happy. Her eyes popped wide and her finger popped up. "Ah!"

"Ma'am?"

"Start anywhere! In the middle. At the end. It doesn't matter. Just start. And once you start, weave your way back. Or forward. Don't worry about where—just start."

. . .

Ms. Miller made it sound so easy, but it was Kandi who made me think I should actually figure out a way to do it.

"Lincoln! Lincoln, wait!" she called, catching up to me on my way to Brookside.

It was a little strange to be happy to see her. Might've had something to do with the way she'd brought Isaac and me into playing four square again at lunch and made sure no one cheated us. I'd made it to first square for three whole serves, something that qualified as a miracle.

And a happy one at that.

She got straight to the point. "I wasn't going to tell you, but I think you should know—Colby showed around your essay while you were out with Ms. Miller today."

"What?"

"She said you must be too embarrassed to write about your Thanksgiving."

"What?"

"I told her to shut up and mind her own business."

I felt like I'd been put in an alternate universe, what with Kandi tellin' someone else to mind their own business and all. But before I could get my bearings, she said, "Are you blocked?"

"Blocked?"

"You know—when a writer can't figure out what to write, they call that being blocked." I didn't say anything, so she went on. "I'd be blocked, too, because I had the worst Thanksgiving ever. But you know what? I'm not writing about that. I'm writing about a made-up Thanksgiving. The decorations are great, the food is delicious, everyone's happy and having a good time. . . . Fiction is fun, and I totally see why you do it."

"You been readin' up about bein' a writer?"

"How'd you know?"

"Well, you know way more about it than I do."

We walked along until what I was thinking finally popped out. "Isaac told me about your ma. I'm sorry." I slid a look her way. "I'm guessin' that's why you had a bad Thanksgiving?"

She nodded, and her eyes got all glassy. "I'm just trying to do what she said: keep my chin up, remember that life is precious, and be a force for good in the world." She burst into tears. "But it's so hard! Sometimes it's just so hard."

Talk about unexpected. I stopped walking and stared.

Kandi wiped her eyes on her sleeve and sat down on a walkway step, her arms propped against her legs, her head sagging like she was just too tired to carry on. "People don't know what it's like," she choked out. "They just don't."

I sat beside her. I couldn't claim to know what it was really like, but just the thought of losing my ma put a rock in my throat. And it was coming to me clearer now that all this time I'd figured Kandi was one thing when it was turning out that she was another.

Finally I ventured, "Maybe you've been workin' so hard

at hiding what you're going through that folks have no idea, and no way of understandin' it."

She turned her weepy eyes on me. "Isn't that what you do?"

The truth in that was undeniable, but I denied it just the same. "No!"

She stared at me, then shook her head and wiped away her tears. "Never mind. Sorry." She stood up. "I've got to go."

She was already hurrying off. "Wait!" I called, chasing after her.

"It's okay, Lincoln. I had a little breakdown. Sorry. I'm fine."

"But—"

"Look, you don't want to talk about yours, I don't want to talk about mine. And even if I did, the truth is, nobody really cares."

My mouth shot open. "I do!"

The words stunned me, but there they were, stopping Kandi in her tracks while they shot a bolt of fear through my heart.

"What did you say?" she asked.

I wanted to run.

Hide!

My heart was galloping in my chest. My mouth was dry. But I could see now that being brave—truly brave— was about more than facing off with Troy, or derelicts at the Laundromat, or even Cliff.

It was about facing off with the truth.

So I stood by my words. "I do," I said, then looked at her square-on. "Writing about some phony Thanksgiving isn't gonna make anyone know what you're goin' through. And you're right—I've been doin' the same thing as you." I took a deep breath. "I love writin' stories, and I'm gonna keep writin' stories. But I'm starting to see that there's a time for stories and there's a time for truth, and I'm thinkin' this is a time for truth. So how about we make a deal: you write about your real Thanksgiving, and I write about mine."

She looked at me for an endless minute. "You're serious?"

I was sweatin' bullets, but I held my ground with a nod.

"Deal," she said. Then she stuck out her hand.

And I shook it.

(51) Full Circle

After Kandi went her way and I went mine, I started losing my nerve. I wanted to hold up my end of the deal, but . . . how could I ever explain my Thanksgiving?

How could I write about my secret life?

I thought about it the whole rest of the way to Brookside.

I thought about it when Geri said, "Good afternoon, Lincoln! Isn't it a lovely day?" as I signed in.

I thought about it when Suzie York asked me, "Do you know how to get out of here?" and Debbie Rucker called, "What is your name?" and Alice said, "Why, hello, sweet pea," and grabbed for my backside.

I thought about it when Teddy C wolf-whistled at Gloria, and when Ma gave me one of her sweet smiles and asked if I was wantin' a snack. I thought about it when I saw that there was a new oldie in Room 102 who had the window-side bed, instead of Wilhelmina.

I thought about it as I passed by Droolin' Stu, and when June and Linda shouted for somebody to make Paula quit tapping.

But how could folks understand if I *didn't* find a way to explain? How could they understand why living in a place with no heat and a sagging floor or sitting up all night with a dying stranger were things to be thankful for, if I didn't explain?

I sat at my table and pulled out my notebook and thought about it for a long time. There was so much stewin' around in my brain. So many *ingredients* in the story. Some sour, some sweet, some salty, some spicy . . . I wasn't sure what to put in.

Or, especially, what to leave out.

And where in the world should I start? I couldn't explain Thanksgiving without explaining stuff that happened before. It wouldn't make any sense! But how far back did I have to go? A week? Two? Back to zombie chicken? Back to the first time the Psychic Vampire struck? Back to when we moved? Back to *why* we moved? It all tied together, and none of it made sense standin' alone.

So . . . where to start?

I was deep into stirring my mental stew when a sound came out of one of the oldies' rooms.

A warbly sound.

Singing.

I snapped to attention and turned away quick, knowin' what was comin' next.

Everyone knew what was comin' next.

Even the oldies who couldn't seem to remember anything else knew what was comin' next.

"Stop her!" Teddy C cried.

"Not again!" Pom-Pom Pam wailed.

But there she was.

Ms. Miller's voice popped into my head—*Start anywhere! In the middle. At the end. It doesn't matter*—and just like that, my pencil took off writing.

Ruby Hobbs came out of her room, dancing and singing, buck naked, again. . . .

About the Author

Wendelin Van Draanen is the author of many award-winning and beloved books, including *Flipped, Swear to Howdy, The Running Dream*, the Sammy Keyes mystery series, the Shredderman quartet, and the Gecko & Sticky books. Read more about her books at WendelinVanDraanen.com or follow her on Twitter at @WendelinVanD.

Wendelin lives in central California with her husband and two sons. Her hobbies include the "three R's": reading, running, and rock 'n' roll.